'I'm n **motion—** **need a PA, and you** **into the role or I will have to consider my options.'**

'You'll fire me?'

She felt the knight sweep towards her. Click, click, click. He knocked away her pawn, and of course it was checkmate, but instead of saying nothing, instead of pleading her case, Lavinia refused to give him the satisfaction. Rather, she blinded him with a smile and accepted defeat with grace. 'I'd love to accept the role.'

'Good. Move your things out to the main office,' Zakahr said, 'then go through your diary and cancel your social life.' He was completely immutable. 'For now your time is mine.'

Carol Marinelli recently filled in a form where she was asked for her job title and was thrilled, after all these years, to be able to put down her answer as 'writer'. Then it asked what Carol did for relaxation, and after chewing her pen for a moment Carol put down the truth—'writing'. The third question asked, 'What are your hobbies?' Well, not wanting to look obsessed or, worse still, boring, she crossed the fingers on her free hand and answered 'swimming and tennis'. But, given that the chlorine in the pool does terrible things to her highlights, and the closest she's got to a tennis racket in the last couple of years is watching the Australian Open, I'm sure you can guess the real answer!

Carol also writes for
Mills & Boon® Medical™ Romance!

THE DEVIL WEARS KOLOVSKY

BY
CAROL MARINELLI

© Carol Marinelli 2012

All the characters in this book have no existence outside the imagination of the author, and have no relation whatsoever to anyone bearing the same name or names. They are not even distantly inspired by any individual known or unknown to the author, and all the incidents are pure invention.

® and TM are trademarks owned and used by the trademark owner and/or its licensee. Trademarks marked with ® are registered with the United Kingdom Patent Office and/or the Office for Harmonisation in the Internal Market and in other countries.

First published in Great Britain 2011
Harlequin Mills & Boon Limited,
Eton House, 18-24 Paradise Road, Richmond, Surrey TW9 1SR

© Carol Marinelli 2011

ISBN: 978 0 263 88631 3

Harlequin Mills & Boon policy is to use papers that are natural, renewable and recyclable products and made from wood grown in sustainable forests. The logging and manufacturing process conform to the legal environmental regulations of the country of origin.

Printed and bound in Spain
by Litografia Rosés, S.A., Barcelona

THE DEVIL WEARS KOLOVSKY

CHAPTER ONE

ZAKAHR could have walked, but he chose not to.

The offices of the House of Kolovsky were, after all, just a short stroll from the luxury hotel that was for the next few weeks Zakahr Belenki's home.

Or, to avoid the press, he could have taken a helicopter for the short hop across the Melbourne skyline.

Except he had long dreamt of this moment.

This moment of the future was one that had sustained Zakahr through a hellish youth—and now, finally, the future was today.

His driver, on Zakahr's instruction, took the long route from the hotel, the blacked-out windows of the sleek limousine causing heads to turn as it made its way through the smart streets lined with galleries and boutiques. As instructed, the driver slowed down at the original House of Kolovsky boutique. The cerulean blue building with the Kolovsky gold logo was familiar, and its wares were desired worldwide. The window display was, as always, elegantly simple—swathes of heavy silk, and one large opal that shimmered in the morning light. Aesthetically it was beautiful, but as always, wherever this sight greeted him on his travels, Zakahr tasted bile.

'Drive on.'

His driver obliged. A few moments later they pulled up outside the offices of the House of Kolovsky, and the moment was Zakahr's.

Cameras were aimed for their shot, and for once he didn't mind. Impossibly wealthy, and with brooding good-looks, he had dated many of Europe's most beautiful and famous women. His heartbreak reputation had been exposed and examined often in the glossies. Though Zakahr usually abhorred the invasion of his privacy, here, on the other side of the world, and especially *this* morning, it did not faze him, and a wry smile was contained as he thought of the Kolovskys watching the news as they ate breakfast.

He hoped they choked.

Questions were hurled, cameras flashed, and microphones were pushed towards him.

Was the House of Kolovsky being taken over by this European magnate? Or was he here covering while Aleksi Kolovsky honeymooned?

Had he enjoyed the wedding?

Was he a relation?

Where was Nina, the matriarch?

What was his interest in Kolovsky?

That was a question with merit. After all, this fashion industry icon was but loose change to a portfolio like Belenki's.

Zakahr made no comment, and neither would he later.

The facts would soon speak for themselves.

The sun beat on the back of his head. His grey blood-shot eyes were hidden behind dark glasses, his lips were pressed together, his expression unreadable, but he was an imposing sight.

A head above everyone, he was broad-shouldered too. His skin was pale, beautifully clean-shaven, and his black hair was short and neat, but despite the immaculate suit, the glint of an expensive watch and the well-heeled shoes, there was an air of the untamed to him—a restlessness beneath the sleek exterior that had the journalists holding back just a touch, with an unusual hesitancy to push for answers. Because no one wanted to be singled out by this man. No one wanted that unleashed power aimed solely at them.

He strode through the street and then up the steps, scattering the press, pushing the golden revolving doors. Zakahr was in.

Perhaps he ought to stand and relish this moment, because finally all this was his. Except there was a hollow feeling inside Zakahr. He relished challenges—had come ready to fight—yet when his identity had been revealed the House of Kolovsky had been handed to him on a plate, and it was now for Zakahr to decide what to do with it.

He sensed the unease of everyone around him.

It did not move him.

'Mr Belenki.'

The greeting followed him. The lift doors were waiting open and he stepped inside. The lift glided up.

He sensed trepidation here too, as he walked out on to

the floor that contained his office. As surely as if it had been pumped through the air-conditioning he could feel it—in the thick carpets, the walls, behind every door as he walked down the corridor. And they had every right to be nervous. Zakahr Belenki had been called in, and in the business world that heralded change.

No one outside family knew who he *really* was.

Zakahr headed to his office. He had been here several times now. Just never as Chief.

He opened the heavy wooden doors, ready to claim his birthright, but his moment was broken as he stepped into darkness. Zakahr frowned as he turned on the lights, and then his jaw clenched in anger—there were no staff to greet him, the blinds were not drawn, the computers were off.

Perhaps the Kolovskys thought they were having the last laugh?

Aleksi had at the weekend married his PA, Kate, but he had assured Zakahr that the last few weeks had been spent training her replacement—except there was no one here.

He headed for a desk, picked up a phone, ready to ring and blast at Reception to get someone up here. But the door opened again, and Zakahr stood, silently fuming, as a stunning blonde came in, wafting fragrance, carrying a large takeaway coffee.

She walked past him to a small office off the main suite, put her drink on the desk, and gave him a quick 'Sorry I'm late' as she slipped off her jacket and turned the computer on. 'I'm Lavinia,' she added.

'I know,' Zakahr said, because he had seen her at his

brother's wedding on Saturday, and hers was a face men noticed and remembered. She had huge blue eyes and a tumble of blonde hair, achieving a look both glamorous and pretty—though Lavinia wasn't looking anything like as amazing as she had at the wedding. There were dark smudges under her eyes, and an air of weariness about her that rather suggested she was more ready for bed than work.

'Is this how you make a good first impression?' Zakahr asked, used to groomed, beautiful staff members who faded into the background—not someone who burst into a room then pulled out a large magnifying mirror from her drawer and proceeded to put make-up on at her desk.

'Give me two minutes,' Lavinia said, unashamedly applying foundation and rather skillfully, Zakahr noticed, erasing all shadows from under her eyes, 'and then I'll make a good impression!'

He couldn't believe her audacity. 'Where is the PA?'

'She got married on Saturday,' Lavinia said.

She was working on her eyes now, her brush loaded with grey. Given Zakahr had been at the wedding, she must have thought her response humorous, because she gave a little laugh at the end of her sentence. As she layered mascara, she told him the necessary truth.

'The stand-in that Kate trained left in tears on Friday and said she was never coming back.'

She wasn't about to sweeten things for him—the House of Kolovsky had been in chaos since the news had got out that Zakahr Belenki was taking over, and if this man really thought he was going to walk in and find order then he was about to find out otherwise.

Lavinia knew he was irritated at her putting on her make-up but what choice did she have? In less than an hour they would be leaving for the airport, and it was essential that she looked the part. But even if none of her previous bosses—Levander, Aleksi or Nina—would have had it any other way, Zakahr was beyond irritated by her actions.

'Did Kate sit at her desk to do her face?'

'Kate,' Lavinia said, with just a hint of ring to her tone, 'wasn't exactly hired for her looks.'

He heard the edge to her voice, and suppressed a smirk at her clear annoyance. Kate was the absolute opposite of Lavinia, and it must surely eat away at this stunning specimen that an overweight, rather plain single mum had married the prize that was Aleksi Kolovsky!

'There's clearly more to Kate than looks,' Zakahr quipped. And, because he just couldn't resist, he added, 'After all, she married the boss!'

He watched the blusher brush pause over her cheek for a second, then she carried on rouging her cheeks.

'Where are *your* staff?' Lavinia frowned, peering over his shoulder as if she expected someone to appear.

'Unfortunately for me you *are* my staff.'

'You didn't bring anyone with you?' The surprise was evident in her voice—she had read up on him, of course. Zakahr Belenki had interests all over Europe. His team swept in on ailing businesses that glinted with potential gold, injecting massive doses of cash to keep them afloat, moving in like a cuckoo, and taking prime place in the newly lucrative nest. And even though Kolovsky was far from ailing, even though Lavinia secretly knew he was here for rather more personal reasons, it was quite unthinkable that he was here alone. 'You haven't brought your team?'

Her question was a pertinent one. His own staff *had* been bemused that he would travel to Australia without them—to them he was assessing the viability of a company. Why wouldn't he bring his team? But Zakahr was a leader. He never displayed weakness, and Kolovsky was his only one. He was not about to explain to his staff why this trip was personal. Still, Zakahr wasn't about to discuss it with Lavinia either, so instead he told her to bring him coffee, then stalked into his office and slammed the door.

Loudly.

Lavinia had worked for both Levander and Aleksi Kolovsky prior to Zakahr, so a slamming door barely made her blink.

Sitting at her desk, all she wanted to do was close her eyes and sleep. It hadn't made the best impression that she was late, but had Zakahr stopped to ask he might have found out the reason—it had truly been the weekend from hell. Propping up Nina at Aleksi's wedding had been the easy part.

On Friday her little half-sister had been moved into foster care, and though Lavinia was beyond relieved that finally action had been taken—Lavinia had actually engineered it—it hadn't been as swift as she had hoped. Instead of Rachael being moved into Lavinia's care she had been placed in a foster home, and the authorities were now assessing the situation.

The true precariousness of Rachael's future had hit hard, and Lavinia had spent three sleepless nights, worrying not just about the future but about how Rachael was coping at the foster home—how the little girl felt sleeping in a strange bed, in a strange home, with strange people.

Even if there was little Lavinia could actually do for Rachael at the moment, even if she could only console herself that at least the little girl was safe, the last place Lavinia wanted to be was here—and if it had been on any other day she would have rung in sick.

Except whom could she ring?

The oh-so-efficient temporary PA Kate had trained had thrown in the towel on the eve of the wedding, Aleksi was on his honeymoon, the other Kolovsky brothers had long since washed their hands of the place, and Nina—*poor* Nina—on finding out the news as to just who Zakahr Belenki was, was now in a private psychiatric hospital.

With the authorities examining Lavinia's suitability to parent, more than ever she needed a stable job, and with that thought in mind, instead of not showing up, Lavinia had showered and pulled on the clothes she had set out the previous night—a dark cami and a gorgeous, if rather short in the skirt, black suit. She had put on her favourite black suede high-heeled shoes, which *always* kicked off an outfit, and had somehow arrived a mere five minutes late—or, as she would point out later, fifty-five minutes early. Most office jobs started at nine!

Not that Zakahr Belenki had thanked her for her effort!

Lavinia poked her tongue out at his closed door.

He was more arrogant than his brothers combined—and that was saying something. She knew who he was! Knew, despite his name, that he was actually a Kolovsky—that he was Nina and Ivan's secret son.

Not that he could find out that she knew.

Happy with her face, Lavinia opened up her computer, ran her eyes over the schedule for the day. Even if she and Kate, the old PA and now Aleksi's bride, had clashed at times, how she wished she were here to sort this out.

Lavinia wore the title of Assistant PA, but was aware she had been hired more as an attractive accessory—a bright and breezy attractive accessory—which was an essential role within Kolovsky. Now, though, the team Ivan had built had, since his death, been slowly dismantled, and that combined with the astonishing news that Zakahr hadn't brought his impressive team left Lavinia with a heavy weight of responsibility.

She shouldn't care, of course.

Lavinia was well aware that some of the minor directors would be only too happy to have their own PAs loaned out to Zakahr—who in this building *didn't* want a direct route to the mysterious new boss?

Lavinia.

She didn't want it, but she had it.

And, like it or not, till Zakahr understood its complicated workings, the smooth running of Kolovsky fell to Lavinia.

She was quite sure people would say she was being grandiose—as if the House of Kolovsky needed Lavinia to survive! Lavinia knew in her heart that it didn't—but some things mattered, they really mattered, and without her inner knowledge certain things that mattered simply wouldn't get done.

Lavinia rested her head on the desk and closed her eyes.

In a minute she would lift it.

In a minute she would force a dazzling smile, would inject some lightness into her face and make them both coffee. Hopefully she and Zakahr could start over again.

She just needed a minute…

'Lavinia!'

This time she jumped!

As Zakahr had intended! Given that he had buzzed her, given that he had called her twice, given that she was asleep at her desk!

She jerked awake at the sound of his voice behind her, felt his brimming anger as strongly as the heavy scent of his cologne, and was tempted just to get her bag and head for home rather than follow his instruction.

'Could you and your hangover please join me in my office?'

CHAPTER TWO

LAVINIA was beyond embarrassed.

She sat at her desk, scalding in her own skin for a full minute, before she could even think of going back out there.

Her first day with her new boss and he'd found her not daydreaming, not dozing, but fast asleep at her desk. Lavinia was used to bouncing back, and she normally did so with a bright smile, but she didn't even try to summon one as she headed for the gallows.

'I'm sorry, Zak…' She walked into his office where he sat, but her voice trailed off when he gestured her to sit and she realised he was on the phone, talking in Russian. Whatever he was saying, Lavinia was quite sure that it wasn't complimentary

His voice was rich and low. He did not shout—there was no need to. There was a ring of confidence and strong assertion behind each word, and she was quite sure this was a man who rarely had to repeat himself.

He was incredibly good-looking, but that was pretty much the norm around here—he was no better than his brothers.

Actually, he *was*, Lavinia conceded.

As if God had made him perfect and then, happy with the formula, had kept on going. There was a salient beauty to him—one that demanded closer inspection—and, just as she would examine the shots of a new Kolovsky model, Lavinia briefly scanned his features. There was rare perfect symmetry to his bone structure, and his high cheekbones and straight Roman nose were a photographer's dream, or nightmare. For not for a second could Lavinia imagine him posing for the camera. There was nothing compliant about those grey eyes, no *give* in his demeanour. Normally she could sum a person up easily, but she was struggling to do so with Zakahr—especially now he had caught her looking.

His eyes held hers as he hung up the phone, and Lavinia felt a warmth spread over her cheeks as he refused to drop his gaze. Rarely—very rarely—it was Lavinia who looked away first, Lavinia who broke a silence that appeared to be only uncomfortable to her.

'I'd like to apologise for before—I didn't get any sleep last night, you see…'

'Are you fit to work?' Zakahr did not care for excuses, and he cut right in. 'Yes or no?'

'Yes.' Lavinia bristled as he refused her attempt to explain.

He stood, leaving her sitting, and went to make the coffee—it was the only way he would ensure it got done. Zakahr was in fact the one battling a hangover. Aleksi's wedding had been hell. He had done the right thing by the man who had tried to do the same for him, but as soon as he'd been able to Zakahr had got out of there and away from the woman he loathed.

He had done everything he could during the service not to look at Nina, the woman who was by biology only his mother, to just ignore her—not to care. Since finding out he was her son Nina had been admitted to a plush psychiatric hospital.

Karma, Zakahr thought darkly.

There was a saying he had learnt as a child—as the call, so the echo. How good he should feel that it was Nina institutionalised now, and that it was he running his parents' empire. It should have been a feeling to savour—only yesterday had found him sitting in an anonymous taxi, staring at the hospital, trying to brace himself to go in.

There was so much to say, so much she *deserved* to hear in a long-awaited confrontation—except, hearing how ill she was, at the final hurdle Zakahr had balked with rare charity, unable to add to her pain.

He had ordered a taxi to the casino, consoled himself that if he chose, soon there would be no House of Kolovsky, soon he could walk away with the name erased and pretend it had never existed—as his parents had done to him. Zakahr had tried to lose himself in noise and stunning women, yet despite his intentions nothing had appealed, and he had spent the night back at the hotel, dousing the bitter churn of emotion in his stomach with hundred-year-old brandy.

And now he was making his assistant coffee!

Seething, he handed her a cup. She tasted it and then screwed up her face and moaned about too much sugar.

He should, Zakahr realised, fire her on the spot.

Just tell her to get out.

Except despite her total lack of professionalism, despite her possibly being the worst Assistant PA in memory, for a little while at least he needed her. Begrudgingly. Extremely begrudgingly. Aleksi had given him a password—one that supposedly accessed all areas—but he had to get in to the system first!

'What is the password?' Zakahr asked. 'For the computer?'

'H-o-K.' Lavinia said, and when that didn't work for him she elaborated. 'The *o* is lower case.'

He shot her a look. 'I want to address everyone to-gether this morning,' Zakahr said. 'Then I want you to arrange fifteen-minute blocks for everyone from cleaner to top designer. After lunch I want the first one at my desk—you co-ordinate it. I want their history file in front of me…'

'You can't.' She watched his lips purse a touch—presumably *can't* was a word rarely said to Zakahr—but he really couldn't. 'We have dignitaries arriving. King Abdullah's daughter—she's coming for a fitting.'

'And?' Zakahr shrugged.

'Once a month or so we have an esteemed bridal guest—a Kolovsky always greets her at the airport and brings her back here…'

'Here?' Zakahr frowned—because surely they would head straight for a hotel?

'Here,' Lavinia confirmed. 'Because this is the moment she's been dreaming of.' He was far too male to understand. 'Anyway, she's hardly been cooped up in Economy. She will have been in their own jet. But someone high up has to greet them—it's what happens, what's expected.'

'The designer can go,' Zakahr dismissed, but when Lavinia still stood there he offered rare compromise. 'You go—if you have to.'

Lavinia ignored this. 'And then, as their host, you will invite her to dinner later in the week, and if their stay has been satisfactory you and your guest will be invited by her family to dinner...' She frowned for a minute. 'I think it's that way around—yes, in a few days she'll ask you to dinner to thank Kolovsky for its hospitality. She's here for a couple of weeks, as the wedding is only a couple of months off.' She saw him frown. 'There are normally a number of trips—Jasmine's doing it all in one.'

'The designers can take care of that side of things.'

'The designers are busy designing.' Lavinia rolled her eyes with impatience. 'The design team will be working day and night on the first designs...'

'I have more important things to do than meet some spoiled princess at the airport.'

'Fine.' Lavinia shrugged. 'Then so do I.' She turned to go, then changed her mind. 'These things matter, Zakahr.' He was working on the computer and didn't look up, and though in truth it wasn't Lavinia's problem, on her previous bosses' behalf it incensed her. 'This is the biggest day of the Princess's life we've been entrusted with. It's her *wedding*!' Lavinia said.

But that word clearly didn't move him, and if he didn't care then neither should she—except Lavinia did.

'I've got a lot going on in my life right now, Zakahr.

And, just for the record, I *didn't* race to get here because the new head of Kolovsky was taking office, I *didn't* sit putting on my make-up to impress *you*—I'm here and ready because I knew that the Princess had to be met. I'm not at my best with our international guests—Kate hated sending me. I forget things, I talk too much, or I show the soles of my feet and such. But I turned up today to try to do what is expected, because that's what Kolovsky is about—beautiful gowns, beautiful women, and at the top of the food chain those blasted wedding gowns.'

He just sat there. Zakahr did not need to be told how things were done by some Assistant PA who fell asleep at her desk. Except he knew he just had been. She was a strange mix, Zakahr decided. Disorganised, yet conscientious. There was also a brazenness to her—a boldness in her slender stature as she awaited his response, hand on hip, toes resisting tapping. Still he said nothing.

'Fine,' she shrilled to the cold silence. 'I'll go myself.'

But first she had to make a phone call…

Back at her desk, Lavinia checked the Princess's flight details, and that the cars were all ready, and waited anxiously for the clock to edge to nine before picking up the phone and dialling.

Ms Hewitt, Rachael's case worker, sounded more angry than exasperated. 'I spoke with you on Friday. You cannot ring in for daily checks—you are *not* her next of kin.'

'I'm trying to be, though.' Lavinia resisted the urge

to say something smart, knowing that she needed these people to be on her side. 'I just want to know that she's okay, and to find out when I can see her.'

'Rachael's father is visiting her on Wednesday evening, and again on Sunday. Really, it's very unsettling for Rachael to have so many visitors.'

'She's my half-sister,' Lavinia bristled. 'How can it be *unsettling* for her to see me?'

'I'll speak with her carers and see if we can arrange something.'

'And that's it?' Lavinia asked. 'Can I at least have a phone number so that I can ring her?'

'We'll contact you if we need to.' Ms Hewitt would not be swayed. 'I'll see if I can arrange a visit.'

Lavinia somehow managed to thank her, then replaced the phone and buried her head in her hands. She hated the lack of speed—couldn't stand what was happening to Rachael—and knew that Kevin, Rachael's father, was still probably dredging up every piece of dirt he could on Lavinia. He'd done everything he could to shut her out of the little girl's life. Maybe it was better that she was at work, because otherwise she'd be standing outside the kindergarten, waiting for Rachael to arrive, and that wouldn't go down well. Lavinia knew she had to stay calm. Had to accept that nothing was going to happen fast—and that she had to prove she was the responsible one.

'Sorry to inconvenience you with work.'

Lavinia looked up to the owner of the voice that dripped sarcasm. He was holding out her jacket, and she didn't even attempt to explain herself. She knew how bad this looked. Instead she just took her jacket and clipped ahead, trying to switch her mind to the job, to being the happy, outgoing person she was at work, whatever the problems in her private life.

They used the rear entrance. A huge limo swallowed them up, with another following to accommodate the royal entourage, and they headed for the airport as Lavinia filled him in as best she could on Princess Jasmine's details. Even Zakahr's eyes widened when she told him what this gown and the dresses for the bridesmaids would be costing King Abdullah.

No wonder Kolovsky, despite everything, was still riding high.

For Zakahr, it was in fact a relief to get out of the office—to get away from the scent of Kolovsky, the surroundings—and for the first time since he had taken over he felt the creep of doubt. He had given himself a month to come to a decision. He was starting to wonder if he could stand to be there for even a week.

For years he had watched the House of Kolovsky from a distance, researching them thoroughly. Levander, Ivan's illegitimate son, had been brought over from Russia as a teenager and given the golden key to Kolovsky. There was no mention of Riminic, Nina and Ivan's firstborn.

Riminic Ivan Kolovsky they had named their baby, as was the Russian way—Riminic, son of Ivan—then at two days old they had taken him to Detsky Dom. Some orphanages were good, but Nina and Ivan had not chosen well. The Kolovsky name meant only hate to Zakahr.

At thirteen he had left the orphanage and had done what he had to to survive on the streets. At seventeen he had been given a chance—shelter, access to a computer, to a different path. Discarding his birth name, he had followed that path with a vision—and that vision included revenge.

As rumours had escalated that Levander had been raised in Detsky Dom, of course the House of Kolovsky had rapidly developed a social conscience, raising great sums for orphanages and street children.

Zakahr had been doing it since his first pay cheque.

And so he had made contact—attending a charity ball Nina had organised as guest speaker, telling the glamorous audience the true hell of his upbringing and his life on the streets. Nina had been sipping on champagne as she had unwittingly met her son.

'It's not just a gown.'

Lavinia dragged him from his thoughts. She was still in full flood, Zakahr realised. She'd probably been talking for five minutes and he hadn't heard a word!

'It's the experience, it's working out the exact colour scheme, it's watching how she walks, her figure, her personality—that's why she has to come to us. For the next few days the Princess will be the sole focus of our designers. Every detail has to be sorted out while she's here. The team will be in regular contact afterwards, of course—and then a week before the wedding our team will fly to her and take care of everything. Hair, make-up—the works. All the Princess will have to do is smile on the day.'

'And how many weddings?' Zakahr asked. 'How often do we have to do this?'

'Once, sometimes twice a month,' Lavinia said, and

then, when she saw his face tighten, it was Lavinia who couldn't resist. 'And what with it coming in to spring in Europe we're exceptionally busy now. You'll be doing this a lot.'

'Great,' he muttered. Talking weddings was so *not* Zakahr.

They sat in silence, and the car was so lovely and warm, and she was just so, so tired, that Lavinia leant back in the sumptuous leather. She wasn't at her desk now, so she did what she would have done had it been any of her old bosses there, and closed her eyes.

Even if she wasn't quite what Zakahr was used to, he begrudgingly admired her complete lack of pretence. Rather more privately, after another sleepless night, he felt like doing the same, but instead he took the opportunity for closer inspection.

She really was astonishingly pretty—or was *attractive* the word? Zakahr couldn't decide. Her jacket was hanging up, her arms lay long and loose by her sides, she had wriggled out of her stilettos, and sat with her knees together and her slender calves splayed like a young colt. Though there was so much on his mind, Zakahr wanted a moment's distraction—and she was rather intriguing. He actually wanted to know more about her.

'How long have you worked for Kolovsky?'

'A couple of years,' Lavinia said with her eyes still closed. 'I did a bit of modelling for them, but I had an extra olive in my salad one day and Nina said I would be better suited in the office.' She opened one eye. 'I'm aesthetically pleasing, apparently, but I'm just not thin enough to model the gowns.'

She was *tiny*! Well, average height. But her waist could be spanned by his hand, her legs were long and slender, her clavicles two jagged lines. Zakahr, who trusted his personal shopper to sort out his own immaculate wardrobe, realised he knew very little about the industry he had taken on.

'What did you do before that?' Zakahr asked her once more closed eyes.

'Modelling—though nothing as tasteful as Kolovsky. It wasn't my proudest period.'

Zakahr didn't say anything.

Lavinia just shrugged. 'It paid the rent.'

It had more than paid the rent.

Hauled out of school by her raging mother one afternoon, the sixteen-year-old Lavinia had become the breadwinner. She had wanted to finish school, had been bright enough to go university—and though she hadn't known what she wanted to be at the time, she had known what she didn't want!

Lavinia had also been bright enough to quickly realise that her mother had no need to know just how many tips she was making.

For two years she had squirrelled away cash in her bedroom.

At eighteen she had opened a bank account and started studying part-time.

At twenty-two, six months after starting work at the House of Kolovsky, and with the requisite employment history, she had marched into her bank, taken her money and bought her very small home.

A home she now wanted to share with Rachael.

Just the thought of her sister alone, with a stranger getting her ready for kindergarten this morning, had Lavinia jolting awake. Her eyes opened in brief panic and she looked straight into the dark pools of Zakahr's gaze—a dark, assessing gaze that did not cause awkwardness. He didn't pretend he hadn't been watching her sleep, he did not use words, and somehow his solid presence brought comfort.

'Rest,' Zakahr said finally.

Only now she couldn't. Now she was terribly aware of him, felt a need to fill the silence. But he was staring out of the window, his expression unreadable, and Lavinia was filled with a sudden urge to tell him she knew who he was, to drop the pretence and find out the truth.

The drive took a good thirty minutes, and was one Zakahr had made a few times in the past months as he had slowly infiltrated Kolovsky. Each time he'd left Australia his heart had blackened a touch further at realising just how lavishly his family had lived all these years while leaving him to fend for himself.

'It's just coming up…'

Zakahr frowned as Lavinia interrupted his dark thoughts.

'Where Aleksi's accident happened…'

There wasn't much to show for it—the tree that had crumpled his car simply wore a large pale scar—but it *did* move Zakahr.

A troubled Aleksi had been trying to halt Zakahr in leaving after his speech at the charity ball, unsure as to his own motives, not even realising that the businessman he was dealing with was actually his brother. Something had propelled him to race to the airport in the middle of the night with near fatal consequences. Though little moved Zakahr, Aleksi's plight had. At seven years old Aleksi had uncovered the fact that he had not just one but two brothers in Russia, and he had confronted his father with the truth. Ivan had beaten him badly enough to ensure that it was forgotten. Only the truth had slowly been revealed.

Out of all of them, Aleksi was the only Kolovsky he had any time for.

'Have you known him long?' Lavinia fished, but Zakahr didn't answer. 'I was surprised Iosef wasn't his best man…' Lavinia tried harder '…given they're twins.'

He was, Lavinia decided, the most impossible man—completely at ease with silence, with not explaining himself. He didn't even attempt an evasive answer—he just refused any sort of response.

'Five minutes, Lavinia,' Eddie the driver warned her and, sick of her new boss's silence, Lavinia opened the partition and asked after Eddie's daughter as she pulled out her make-up bag.

'Six weeks to go!' Eddie said.

'Are you excited?' Lavinia asked, and then glanced over to Zakahr. 'Eddie's about to become a grandfather.'

It could not interest Zakahr less, and his extremely brief nod should have made that clear, but Lavinia and Eddie carried on chatting.

'I can't stop my wife shopping—we've got a room full of pink!'

'So it's a girl!'

Lavinia seemed delighted, and Zakahr watched as she snapped into action—touching up her make-up and combing her long blonde hair.

She could feel him watching her, sensed his irritation, and her blue eyes jerked up from the mirror. 'What?'

He shrugged and looked away before he answered. 'I don't like vanity.'

'I'd suggest that you *do*!'

'Pardon?'

'You've dated enough vain women,' Lavinia pointed out. 'According to my impeccable sources.'

'Five-dollar magazines?' Zakahr was derisive, but still he was intrigued. Lavinia wasn't remotely unnerved by him, and it was surprisingly refreshing. 'Are you always this rude to your boss?'

'*Was* I rude?' Lavinia thought about it for a moment. 'Then, yes, I suppose I am. You wouldn't last five minutes in this place otherwise.' She was annoyed now—he just didn't get it. 'And it has nothing to do with my being vain—this isn't *me*!' Lavinia said. 'This is me at work. Do you really think the Princess wants someone greeting her in jeans with oily hair?' She was on a roll now! 'And another thing—while by your calculations I was five minutes late, I was actually fifty-five minutes *early*. Most people start work at nine. And because *work* insists I look the part, when I got to *work* I ensured that I did,' she concluded, snapping closed her lipgloss as the driver opened the car door. Then, having said her piece, she suddenly smiled and did what Lavinia did best—got on with the job. 'Let's go and meet the Princess!'

Zakahr had realised back at the office that it would be extremely offensive for him not to greet the royal guests, and he was more than a little grateful to his dizzy PA for her strong stance. Because it wasn't just the Princess—the King himself was here. Zakahr quickly assessed that one bad word from this esteemed guest and even the great Kolovsky name would be dinted.

Zakahr swung into impressive action—greeting the guests formally in the VIP lounge, and immediately quashing any disappointment that neither Nina nor Aleksi was here to greet them.

Lavinia *was* very good at small talk, Zakahr noted, back in the limousine. She chatted away to the shy Princess and her mother, and very quickly put them at ease. And every layer of lipgloss, Zakahr conceded, was merited—because it was clear the royal family expected nothing less than pure glamour, and Kolovsky could deliver that in spades.

'The team are so looking forward to finally meeting with you,' said Lavinia now.

She was nothing like the pale, wan woman who had stepped into his office this morning. She was effusive, yet professional, and as they stepped out of the limo it was Lavinia who paved the way, speaking in low tones to Zakahr about what was taking place.

'We take them through to the design team now.'

The King remained in the car, his aides in the vehicle behind, and they all waited till they had driven off before the colourful parade made its way to the centre of Kolovsky. Every door required more authorisation, but then they were in.

'Thank you.' Zakahr was not begrudging when praise was due, and as they left the Princess in the design team's skilled hands he thanked Lavinia. 'It would have been unthinkable of me not to greet the King!'

'I know!' She gave him a wide eyed look. 'They don't normally come—the men, I mean. Lucky!'

He didn't know why, but she made his lips twitch almost into a smile. He contained himself as Lavinia showed him the wedding displays, all locked behind glass and beautifully lit. She headed straight for the centrepiece.

'This,' she said, 'is the one they all want. The Kolovsky bridal gown.' He stared at it for a moment. 'Beautiful, isn't it?' Lavinia pushed.

'It's a dress,' Zakahr said, and Lavinia laughed.

'It's *the* dress! It was supposed to be for the Kolovsky daughter, or one of their son's brides—well, that's what Nina and Ivan intended.' She didn't see his face stiffen. 'It's the dress of every woman's dreams,' Lavinia breathed, peering closely and steaming up the glass as she did so. 'It actually *is*,' she added. 'I dreamt about this dress long before I ever saw it.'

Zakahr was not going to stand there and engage in idle chit-chat about a wedding dress, and without a word he walked off. But she caught up with him, trotting along to keep up with his long strides, and—annoyingly for Zakahr—carrying on with her incessant chatter.

'I used to fall asleep dreaming about my wedding, and I swear that was the dress I was wearing—it really is the dress of dreams.'

'You fell asleep dreaming of your *wedding*?' They

were in the lift now, and he couldn't keep the derisive note from his voice.

'I was eight or so!' Lavinia shrugged, then coloured a touch as his eyes assessed her.

'You don't dream of it now?' Zakahr checked, and he watched her ears pinken a fraction.

'Sometimes I do.' She shocked him with her honesty. 'Then the alarm goes off and it's back to the real world.' She gave him a little wink as the lift door opened. 'Or I hit the snooze button.'

Was she being deliberately provocative? Zakahr couldn't be sure, and it irked him. There was an edge to Lavinia—an openness that was inviting, a smile that was beguiling—and yet there was a no-nonsense element to her too, almost a wall. The combined effect, he reluctantly admitted, was intriguing.

'We have much work to do,' Zakahr said as they reached the office suite. 'We'll start the one-on-one interviews tomorrow, but this afternoon I will address everyone—liaise with HR, but I want *you* to arrange it.'

'It's not possible,' Lavinia told him. 'People have meetings scheduled, and there are—'

'Anyone not present has effectively handed in their notice.' He cut her off mid-sentence. He would accept no excuses, and Lavinia's lips pursed as he left her no room for manoeuvre. 'Just do as I ask.'

'The thing is—'

Zakahr halted her. 'The thing is I am in charge now. Whatever your relationship with your previous boss—

disregard it. When I say I want something done, it is not up for negotiation.

'Which night do we dine with the King?'

'Wednesday. But I don't do dinner.' Lavinia shook her head. 'They only trust me with the occasional airport run.'

'Well, for now you do the social side of things too,' Zakahr said. 'You have a promotion.'

'I don't want it,' came her immediate response.

Lavinia loved her job—she'd vied for pole position with Kate at times—but she didn't actually want to do Kate's work. And it wasn't just the fact that she wasn't remotely qualified. There was Rachael, her studies, Nina—just so many demands on her time right now it really was an impossible task.

'You will be remunerated.'

'It's not about money,' Lavinia said. 'I'm busy…'

'Too busy to work?' Zakahr frowned. 'I'm not *offering* you a promotion—I am telling you that I need a PA, and you either step into the role or I will have to consider my options.'

'You'll fire me?'

'If I don't have a PA what is the point of employing her assistant?'

She felt the knight sweep towards her. Click-click: he knocked away her pawn, and of course it was checkmate. But instead of saying nothing, instead of pleading her case, Lavinia refused to give him the satisfaction. Rather, she blinded him with a smile and accepted defeat with grace. 'Congratulations!'

'Pardon?'

She loved that she'd confused him. 'I'd love to accept the role, Zakahr.'

'Good. Move your things out to the main office,' Zakahr said. 'Then go through your diary and cancel your social life.' He was completely immutable. 'For now your time is mine.'

CHAPTER THREE

LAVINIA had never worked harder in such a short space of time.

Firing off e-mails, replying to e-mails, then resorting to repeating—not quite verbatim—Zakahr's warning, she sent a final e-mail with the word 'COMPULSORY' in capitals, and a little red exclamation mark beside it—though she did wrangle from an unwilling Zakahr exclusion for Jasmine's design team. Then she cleared the main function room of a group of sulky models and designers who were trying to prepare for a photoshoot for the sulkiest of them all—Rula, a stunning redhead who was to be the new Face of Kolovsky. Finally checking the PA system, Lavinia had done in an hour what it would take most a full day to achieve.

Not that Zakahr thanked her as she raced back to her office to collect her bag. He merely glanced up as he came in.

'Everything's in place.' Lavinia spritzed her wrists with perfume. 'I'll be back before two.'

'Back from where?'

'Lunch!' From his expression she might just as well have sworn. 'I'm surely entitled to a lunch-break?' In support of her argument, Catering wheeled in a sumptuous trolley of delights for Zakahr, but it did not appease him.

'We will work through lunch,' Zakahr said. 'Come and eat with me.'

'I really can't,' Lavinia said. 'I've got an appointment. A doctor's appointment.' She ran a hand over her stomach and Zakahr pressed his lips together.

She knew every trick, he realized. Knew with just that fleeting gesture no man would pry into women's business—and Lavinia was certainly that: a woman.

'Sorry!' Lavinia added.

She didn't hang around for his reaction. Instead she darted out to the lift, just a little bit breathless at her lie—because if Zakahr knew where she was going on her lunch-break he'd do more than sack her. It was, she knew, the ultimate treachery. He'd go ballistic if he knew where she was heading.

But she couldn't *not* go.

'Hi, Nina.'

Nina didn't look up—she was talking to herself in Russian—but Lavinia hugged her. Trying to keep the shock from her voice, she chatted away—except Lavinia *was* shocked. In a couple of days the other woman had surely aged a decade.

Nina had somehow got through her son's wedding. On day leave from the plush psychiatric hospital, and sedated from strawberry-blonde head to immaculately shod feet, she had worn a smile and a fantastic Kolovsky dress, and with Lavinia's help had managed to get through the service. But clearly the public effort had depleted her.

Her hair hung in rats' tails, her nail polish was chipped, and there was no trace of make-up. The silk she usually wore was replaced by a hospital gown, and all Lavinia knew was that Nina—the real Nina—would absolutely hate to be seen like this.

'I'm going to do your hair, Nina,' Lavinia said, rummaging in her locker and finding some hair straighteners. 'And then I'm going to do your nails.'

Nina made no response. She just sat talking in Russian as Lavinia smoothed out her hair. Only when Lavinia sat and worked on her nails did Nina speak in English—the questions, the statements, always in the same vein. 'He hates me. Everyone hates me.'

'I don't hate you, Nina,' Lavinia responded, as she always had since the day the news had hit.

A terrible day that was etched for ever in her mind.

Aleksi had returned from his accident to find Nina had taken over, and a terrible struggle for power had ensued. Nina had taken advice from Zakahr, who from afar had fed her ideas that would make huge profits but, as Aleksi had pointed out, would also cause Kolovsky's demise.

Then Zakahr had swept in, and for Aleksi realisation had hit: the man toying with Nina was actually his brother.

Lavinia could still recall the moment Nina had found out that Zakahr was her son. She had held Nina as she'd collapsed to the floor while Aleksi had told her in no uncertain terms of what Riminic, the child she had abandoned, had endured in the orphanage, and then in graphic detail what the runaway teenager had gone through to survive on the streets.

'They will never forgive me.' Around and around Nina went.

'Your family just need some time to process things,' Lavinia said patiently. 'Annika has been in to see you, and Aleksi has rung from his honeymoon. I know Levander has been in touch from the UK, and Iosef *has* been in to see you.'

'They are all disgusted with me.'

Lavinia let out a breath and focussed on painting a middle nail. Sometimes she truly didn't know what to say. 'They need time,' she said.

'I had no choice,' Nina pleaded, but Lavinia would not be manipulated. She was used to her mother's ways, and in a lot of things Nina behaved the same.

'There are always choices,' Lavinia said. 'Maybe you made the best decision you could at the time.'

'I should have tried to find him,' Nina said, and Lavinia, who never, ever cried, felt her eyes suddenly well up.

The nails she was trying to focus on blurred, and for a moment she couldn't answer—because, yes, Nina *should* have tried to find him. And, yes, when they were so rich and powerful, surely, *surely* she should have tried to find her son. And it dawned on her, fully dawned, that the brooding, closed-off man she had met this morning was actually the baby Nina had abandoned.

'Why didn't you?' Lavinia couldn't stop herself from asking. 'Why didn't you even try?'

'I saw how everyone hated me when Levander came to Australia—when they found out I knew his mother had died, and that Levander had been raised in Detsky Dom orphanage…'

Lavinia blew her hair upwards. Nina was getting more and more indiscreet, and the rumour that had quietly blown through Kolovsky—that Nina had known all along—was, to Lavinia's horror, confirmed.

'Levander wasn't my blood, and still they hated me. I couldn't face it if they knew there was more—that I had left my own son too.'

'Well, you have to face it.' Lavinia bit down on the sudden white-hot fury that shot through her. 'You have to face it because the truth is here.'

'Does he ask about me?' Nina begged. 'Does Riminic ask about me?'

'Nina…' Lavinia shook her head in exasperation. 'He doesn't have a clue that I know who he really is—to me he's Zakahr Belenki, someone Kolovsky was doing business with, and he's taken over now that Aleksi is working solely on the Krasavitsa fashion line and you are not well. That's all he thinks I know.'

'He is beautiful, yes?' Nina said. 'How could I not see he was my son? How did I look in his eyes and not recognise him?'

'Maybe you were scared to,' Lavinia offered. She glanced up at the clock on the wall. She was loath to leave her because at least Nina was talking now, but she had no choice. 'I have to go, Nina.'

And then, in the midst of her devastation, as always Nina remembered.

'How is your sister?'

Lavinia toyed with whether to tell her or not. She had always confided in Nina, but now it just didn't seem the right time.

'She's doing okay.'

'She likes kindergarten?'

'She does,' Lavinia said quietly, thinking of Rachael's serious little face—a guarded face that rarely smiled. She was reminded of Zakahr.

'You keep fighting for her.'

Nina stroked Lavinia's cheek, and Lavinia truly didn't get it. She had seen the worst of Nina—had heard her bitch and moan, had worked alongside her even as she tried to have Aleksi ousted. With all the shame of her past—the fact she hadn't fought for her own son—there was so much to despise, and yet Nina could be so kind.

'Give her my love.'

'I will.' Lavinia stood up. 'I'd better get back.'

She really *had* better get back—hospital visits didn't really squeeze into lunch-breaks, and she'd have to run through the car park to make it back to the office.

But as she raced out of the lift she saw Zakahr had beaten her to it.

'How was the doctor?' he asked.

'Not great.' Lavinia put on her best martyred face, but instead of being cross with her Zakahr actually wanted to laugh—she was such an actress.

'Poor you,' Zakahr said, and she caught his eye, not sure if he was being sarcastic—not sure of this man at all.

He unsettled her.

All morning he had unsettled her—in a way very few did.

She would *not* be intimidated. Lavinia utterly refused to be. Only it wasn't just that—it was the lack of roaming in those eyes, the stillness in him as he looked not at her, not through her, but *into* her that made her breath quicken, made the ten-second lift-ride down to the main function room seem inordinately long. And when the lift doors opened she forgot to step out.

'After you,' Zakahr said, when she had stood for a second too long.

And because Zakahr didn't know the way to the stage entrance Lavinia had to lead, awkward now, with him walking behind.

'Hopefully everything's in place…' She hung back a touch and walked in step with him, tried to make small talk. But Zakahr, of course, didn't engage in that.

Lavinia was just a little impressed with what she had achieved—and just a little praise would have been welcome. Effectively the place had been put into lockdown, and now, as they stood in the wings, instead of models and the new season's display, it was Zakahr Belenki who was the star of the show, with wary, disgruntled staff waiting to hear their fate.

He wasn't in the least nervous, Lavinia realised, as he leant against the wall reading e-mails on his phone while the head of HR read out his credentials to the tense audience. Even Lavinia had butterflies on his behalf, yet Zakahr was as relaxed as if he were waiting for a bus.

'Hold on a second…' She put her hand up to correct his tie, just as she would have for Aleksi, just as she would have if Nina had had a strap showing as she was about to walk on. But on contact she immediately wished that she hadn't. The simple, almost instinctive manoeuvre was suddenly terribly complicated. She felt his skin beneath her fingers, inhaled the scent of him as she moved in closer, the sheer maleness of him as she moved his tie a fraction to the centre and went to smooth his collar down.

His hand shot up and caught her wrist.

'What are you doing?' Zakahr was the least touchy-feely person on the planet. Flirting, unnecessary touching—he partook in neither. Lavinia seemed a master at both.

'Sorry!' His reaction confused her. There had been nothing flirtatious about her action, but Zakahr seemed less than impressed. 'Sheer habit,' Lavinia explained. Only her voice came out a little higher than normal, and her breath was tight in her chest as those eyes now did roam her body. His hand let go of her wrist, but instead of dropping to his side, the warm, dry hand slid around her neck. Lavinia stood transfixed. For a second she thought he was going to pull her towards him—for a full second she thought she was about to be kissed—but instead his fingers stole down the nape of her neck to the tender skin there, tucked in a label he couldn't even have seen beneath her thick blonde hair. And then he mocked her with a black smile. She could see the flash of warning, and she could see something else too—the danger beneath the slick surface of him.

'That's better,' Zakahr said, his hand still on the back of her neck. 'It was annoying me.'

'I was just…' Lavinia attempted to explain again that she had just been straightening his tie, but her voice faded as Zakahr shook his head.

'No games!' Zakahr said. 'Because you have no idea who you are playing with.'

The applause went up, and without a further word he headed out, leaving Lavinia standing in the wings, her neck prickling from his touch, stunned and unsure as to what had just taken place.

And then he smiled.

A slow smile that moved around the room like the rays of the sun.

Those grey eyes somehow met everyone's, and before he had even opened his mouth the audience was his.

'There is much fear and speculation today,' Zakahr said, his accent more pronounced over the microphone. 'I cannot end the speculation, but I hope to allay your fears.'

He did.

Everyone had a voice, he told his captive audience, and he would listen to each one. He expected the House of Kolovsky to continue to flourish, and was looking forward to getting to know the staff.

A smile of relief swept the room—only it didn't reach Lavinia, and neither did his speech. It was his earlier words that rang in her ears as she watched from the shadow of the wings.

'You have no idea who you are playing with.'

But she did.

Riminic Ivan Kolovsky—a man surely with no allegiance to the empire, a man who had learnt hate from the cradle, a man who had practically warned her himself to steer clear.

She didn't trust him. She wasn't even sure if she liked him. And he was absolutely out of her league. So why, Lavinia asked herself as her hand moved to the back of her neck, as she felt the skin he had branded with his touch, did she really want to know him some more?

CHAPTER FOUR

THERE was no one less fun to work for.

It was straight down to business after yet another sleepless night.

Not only did she have Rachael to worry about, there was now that incident with Zakahr. She *hadn't* been flirting, she'd thought indignantly as she'd lain there. Or maybe she had? Blushing in the darkness, Lavinia had rolled over, replaying that seemingly innocent gesture over and over, replaying: Zakahr's warm fingers on the back of her neck, her being momentarily trapped at his bidding.

Even though she'd hauled herself to work early, Zakahr, of course, was already there. She made him coffee and took it in, but he neither looked up nor thanked her—just asked for some staff files and re-minded her that he wanted to commence interviews at nine. Lavinia rued her night of imaginings—clearly it hadn't troubled him a jot.

Lavinia ached for the old days—gossiping by the coffee machine, chatting with Aleksi. Even Kate would have made things so much more bearable. But with Zakahr it was just work, work, work.

Her lunch break consisted of a mad dash for the vending machine and yet another energy drink.

'Annika's on the line.' When a moment later Zakahr still hadn't picked up his sister's call, Lavinia buzzed him again, and then knocked on his door. 'Annika's on the phone for you.'

'I'm busy with interviews. Who's next?' Zakahr asked, raising an eyebrow at the large energy drink she was carrying. It was Lavinia's third of the day.

'I'm just trying to get hold of her—it should be Alannah Dalton, Head of Retail,' Lavinia said, handing him the file.

'And?' Zakahr asked, because Lavinia's little off-the-record additions were actually spot-on.

'A right old misery. She moans about everything—thinks the whole world's out to get her…' Her voice trailed off, and Zakahr looked up to see that Lavinia's eyes were closed and that despite her make-up there was a sallow tinge to her cheeks.

'Are you going to faint?' He sounded weary at the thought of it.

'No,' Lavinia whispered. 'I'm just…' For an appalling moment she thought she might be sick, but it abated and she took a deep breath, licked very dry lips. The world was swimming back into focus. 'I had no sleep last night.' She saw his jaw tighten. 'I know it's not your problem—it's entirely mine…'

She sat on his large sofa and put her head on her knees for a moment. He just sat at his desk and watched, neither worried nor impressed—if anything, he was bored by the drama of her.

'I'll be fine,' Lavinia said a couple of moments later.

Only she wasn't.

She made it out of his office even as little dots danced before her eyes. She gulped down water, ate four jelly beans and a bag of crisps that had been hiding in her desk, and took a call from Alannah.

Lavinia buzzed Zakahr. 'She's on her way from the boutique. They had an important client.' She didn't actually hear his response, because there was a loud ringing sound in her ears.

When Alannah Dalton didn't appear, and neither did Lavinia respond to his intercom buzzer, Zakahr marched out of his office, less than impressed, to find her once again head-down at her desk.

'I'm not asleep,' Lavinia said without moving. 'And I really am sorry.' She had to tell him—well, not tell him everything, but she had to admit a bit of the truth—it was either that or get fired. 'I've got some personal problems. I hardly had any sleep over the weekend, just worrying, and it was the same last night…'

Now she did lift her head, and Zakahr rather hoped she'd put it down again. Her lips were white, her mascara was sliding down her cheeks, and he was now worried rather than weary. He was used to more staff, used to snapping his fingers and producing solutions, but in a situation of his own making there was no one.

He went to the en suite bathroom, ran water onto a hand towel and brought it back to her. He wasn't entirely convinced by her story, but she was clearly ill, so he took the towel, and she accepted it without thanks, burying her face in it as Zakahr stood silent till finally she came up for air.

'I'll be better tomorrow.' Lavinia was insistent. 'I'll be back to normal.'

'I'll get my driver to take you home—' Zakahr started, but he halted as she winced. The thought of walking, of getting into a car, clearly had her dizzy all over again. 'You need to rest…'

He led her to what had actually been her old office, before Zakahr had insisted on the promotion, and she fell into the familiar cushions with relief. It had never been more blissful to lie down. But now that the world was back in focus embarrassment was seeping in.

'I'm really sorry.' There was colour coming back to her face now, though her make-up was on the towel which she had pressed to her forehead. 'I can explain.'

'Just rest for now,' Zakahr said. Seeing that she was shivering, he did the right thing and took off his jacket and covered her. Then he pulled the blinds. By the time he had finished she was sound asleep.

Zakahr rang down to Reception and had someone sent up to replace Lavinia for the rest of afternoon, while he carried on conducting staff interviews. Alannah Dalton *was* a right old misery, as Lavinia had said.

He was a skilled interviewer, and he listened as the staff ranted and raved, and saved their own skin by blaming others.

He learnt a lot.

Confirmed a lot.

The cracks in Kolovsky had started long before Ivan's death—of course he pursued this, but on too many occasions his mind wandered to the woman asleep next door, no matter how many times he tried to halt it.

'Were there staff favourites?' Zakahr asked them all.

It was as simple as that.

Of course he had to listen to a lot that did not interest him in order to get to the bit that did. It was common knowledge that Lavinia had been sleeping with Aleksi, and maybe Levander too, before him. Lavinia, he was repeatedly told, always kept in with the boss.

Zakahr kept his face impassive as over and over this was reiterated, but he almost felt regret as he realised that the smile he was starting to like, the chatter, the jokes—everything that was Lavinia—wasn't pleasing exclusively to him.

In a break between interviews Zakahr walked into the darkened office and stared down at her for a full moment. With her face relaxed by sleep, her mouth minus the gloss, she looked younger, prettier—innocent, almost.

Though clearly that wasn't the case.

He found her file and bundled it up with a few others, and then he settled back for a read.

She had been hauled in to HR several times—always at another colleague's request—and Kate herself had made a couple of complaints, but there had never been any action taken.

Zakahr was quite sure he knew why.

At five p.m., she stepped into his office, with a red mark from the cushion on the side of her face.

'I don't know what to say!' She handed him his jacket, which he took without a word. 'Thank you, though. I'll see you tomorrow—assuming, of course…' Lavinia tried to keep her voice upbeat, but even she could hear its waver '…that I still have a job?'

'Do you even *want* this job?' Zakahr asked.

'Of course I do,' Lavinia responded immediately—because now more than ever a solid working history was vital.

'Then can I suggest you go home to bed and sleep tonight?' Zakahr said tartly. 'And that you eat something instead of relying on caffeine…' She exasperated him—why, he didn't know. She was too pale, too thin and too careless with herself, and even though it was far from his problem for a moment it felt like it. 'Let's both get something to eat.'

Lavinia shook her head. Because even if she was starving, even if all she'd have the energy to rustle up this evening was egg on toast, the thought of being out with Zakahr—of an evening away from the office, actually talking to him—had her body on instant alert. She'd heeded his warning. She wasn't about to toy with him. His company out of office hours would be perilous at least!

'I'm really not up to a fancy restaurant today—and we're eating out with the King tomorrow. Right now I just want to go home, have a bath, and go to sleep.'

'Home, *eat*, bath and then sleep,' Zakahr said through gritted teeth, not trusting her to do so. Taking it into his own hands, he stood. 'You need to eat, and so do I.'

CHAPTER FIVE

HE TOOK her somewhere very dark, very low-key, and actually rather relaxing.

'How do you know about this place?' Lavinia had grumbled as they'd turned into a back street and he'd led her to what must be one of Melbourne's best-kept secrets. As she slipped into deep velvet seats Lavinia peered around and saw it was filled with the rich and the beautiful. 'I've lived here all my life and didn't know it existed.'

'Concierge,' was Zakahr's concise reply, but then he stopped being her boss for a moment and gave her a brief smile. 'The food is good.'

And she *did* need to eat. She ordered a snow pea and asparagus risotto, which was smothered in pepper and fresh parmesan, and layered butter on a warm roll.

Conversation came easily, and Lavinia surprised Zakahr by tucking in to her food the moment it arrived— and even if she only managed a quarter of the large plate he watched with surprising pleasure as colour came back to her complexion and that sparkle came back to her eyes.

'Better?' Zakahr asked.

'Much,' Lavinia admitted—because the food *had* been lovely, and the company pleasant rather than challenging. Far from feeling awkward, for the first time in ages Lavinia found herself unwinding.

'You need to take better care of yourself.'

'I take very good care of myself,' Lavinia responded, but then relented. 'Usually.'

Zakahr waited for her to elaborate—his skilled interview technique continued long after office hours. He chose to give away little about himself, and the easiest way to accomplish that was to ask about *her* life—but though Lavinia spoke easily about work, weddings and the like, she was surprisingly reticent when it came to her current problems. In fact, when Zakahr subtly asked the nature of her problems, Lavinia turned the question on *him*.

'Just family stuff—but then you'd know all about family dramas, wouldn't you?' She watched his steak knife pause, and after a moment he actually put down the cutlery and took a drink of water before speaking. He was unsure if he'd misheard, because it was such a guarded secret—one the Kolovskys dreaded getting out—surely the Assistant PA couldn't know?

'Do you come from a large family?' Zakahr asked instead of answering.

'I've got a half-sister.' She saw him frown, and realised she was making no sense. And though she was really too weary to explain herself, so much had been bottled inside for so long that Lavinia found herself opening up. 'My mum died last year.'

'I'm sorry,' Zakahr said, as was polite, but Lavinia gave a tight shrug.

'She lived longer than expected,' Lavinia said. 'I'm rather amazed that she made it into her forties—my mum was someone who really didn't take care of herself.' She pushed the risotto around her plate—hungry, but not, angry, but not. Just sharing her burden, just voicing it, might bring fresh perspective.

'What about your father?' Zakahr pushed.

'I don't have a father,' she said. 'Well, I don't…'

'You don't keep in touch?'

'I don't know who he is.' She gave a tight smile that was born from embarrassment. 'Neither did my mother.'

'I see.'

'I doubt it.

'Look.' Lavinia gave up with her food. 'My half-sister is younger than me—*much* younger. She lives with her father and his new partner. It was bad enough leaving her there when my mother was alive—I know what I went through as a child—but now that she's gone…well, I know that Kevin doesn't want her, and nor does his new partner. I'm trying to get custody, but they're opposing it…'

Zakahr looked up, unable to imagine the high-fashion, rather dizzy Lavinia taking on the role of single mum. But since the moment he had met her she had surprised him.

'I thought you said that they didn't want her?' Zakahr frowned. 'What is her name?'

'Rachael, and she's four.' Her tense mouth softened

even as she said the name. 'They *don't* want her. But Mum had a life insurance policy, and there's a small trust for her—they'd get paid. Not a huge amount, but enough to make it worth their while to keep her. They deny it's about money, of course, but I know I'm right.'

'So how do you know that they don't want her? Really know?' Zakahr asked—because he dealt only in fact.

'Her dad's got two older boys who can do no wrong, and his partner's got two little girls from another relationship. And now they've just had a baby of their own.'

'A large blended family,' Zakahr said, but Lavinia screwed up her nose.

'Rachael doesn't fit into the blend,' Lavinia said. 'She's clever, she's a serious little thing, and they just have no time for her. I buy her clothes, but I go there and the girls are wearing them while Rachael's in rags. She spends most of her time in her room.' He saw the flash of tears in her eyes as she took a large gulp of water. 'It's the hardest thing to explain,' Lavinia admitted. 'It's actually *impossible* to explain. I used to see her once a fortnight, and if I argued or pointed anything out—well, I just didn't get to see her the next time.'

'So you've stayed quiet?'

'Do you know how hard it is to stay quiet when you know a child is suffering?'

Zakahr said nothing.

'I arranged some childcare for her—it had a kindergarten programme. I told Debbie…'

'The partner?' Zakahr checked, and Lavinia nodded.

'I told her that it might give her a break, that I knew

Rachael was hard work—I made it sound like I was doing them a favour. But in fact I wanted her away from them, and hopefully for one of the teachers to see what was going on.'

'Which they did?'

'She had some bruises on her arms,' Lavinia said. 'And they were worried about some of the stuff she'd been saying. She was taken into foster care on Friday. I thought I'd get her—I really thought it would be automatic—now I'm being *assessed*.' She shrilled out the word. 'I've got my own record with them,' Lavinia admitted. 'I was bounced in and out of care for most of my childhood—'

'And that goes *against* you?' Zakahr checked. 'You are responsible now—you have a good job...'

'I didn't always,' Lavinia said, and she was so weary with it all, so tired of trying to justify herself, she simply stopped. To Zakahr she would be honest. 'The "modelling" that I used to do—after my mum pulled me out of school at sixteen—I was actually a stripper for a few years. Then I did some dancing...'

'I'm assuming not classical?'

There was nothing derisive in his voice, no shock in his eyes—all he did was listen—so much so that Lavinia even managed a wry smile.

'Steer me away from all poles!' she said to his bland expression. 'I just can't help myself sometimes.'

'You modelled as well?'

'That's how I ended up at Kolovsky—it was a fashion week, the agents were frantic, Kolovsky were a bridesmaid short... It was luck, really.'

'You'd still be dancing without Kolovsky?'

'God, no,' Lavinia said immediately. 'I'd all but given up on Mum by then—I still gave her some money for Rachael, but it all went on gin. I was looking for another job. This one, though, paid far more than I'd dreamed. It was a Godsend.' She caught his eyes. 'I know I haven't made the best impression, but I really do need this job—now more than ever. Two years as Assistant PA, a recent promotion to PA…' She gave a tight smile. 'Well, it beats an unemployed ex-stripper.'

'Have you taken legal advice?'

'What can a lawyer do?' Lavinia asked. 'It's up to the authorities.'

'A lawyer can ask questions.' Zakahr thought for a moment. 'You say Kevin is good with his sons?'

Lavinia nodded.

'So why not Rachael?'

'Maybe he prefers sons…' Lavinia started, then changed her mind. 'He seems to dote on the new baby, though, and she's a little girl.'

'Get advice.'

Lavinia rolled her eyes. It was all very well for Zakahr, with his billions, to suggest a lawyer. 'I'll just keep working on Ms Hewitt!' She smiled over to him, but Zakahr didn't smile back. In fact he was annoyed—not with Lavinia, but with his brothers, with his so-called family.

Hell, he'd known Lavinia a couple of days and already knew her story. She'd been Aleksi's lover—surely he should have sorted this out for her? And what about

Nina? They had lawyers galore at Kolovsky—surely someone could have stepped in?

'You need to speak to someone,' Zakahr said, reluctant to be dragged into a problem that wasn't his, but unable to stay quiet.

'What I need,' Lavinia corrected, 'is to keep my job. So, thank you for listening, and I promise after a good night's sleep I'll be back to my usual self!'

He rather liked her *un*usual self! Still, that wasn't the issue.

'Listen to me, Lavinia. You can't deal with this without a lawyer.'

'I *am* dealing with it,' she insisted. 'I know the system well enough—Ms Hewitt was my own case worker years ago. You know, it really *is* a shame you can't choose your family!' Maybe she should just stay quiet, not admit that she knew, but Lavinia didn't work well being subtle, and frankly she'd had enough of playing games. 'Zakahr—I know who you are.'

'You shouldn't listen to gossip.'

'Everyone's too scared to gossip about *you*,' Lavinia said. 'I was there when Aleksi confronted Nina with the truth that you are in fact her son.'

'Was,' Zakahr corrected.

'*Are*,' Lavinia said.

'They are not my family.'

'So why are you here?' Lavinia challenged. 'If you want nothing to do with them, why are you here?'

'To claim what is rightfully mine,' Zakahr lied; he was hardly going to tell her of his intention to destroy it.

'You could talk to her…' Lavinia knew she was

venturing into dangerous territory—knew this was absolutely not her place—but Nina's devastation was real.
'At least hear what she has to say…'

'I can forgive tardiness, I can forgive rudeness, and I
can accept that in some things for now you know better.'
His voice was like ice. 'But don't *ever* try to advise me
on my family.'

'Fine,' Lavinia said. 'But what gives you the right to
advise on mine?'

'I'm right,' Zakahr snapped.

'So am I!' She reached for her bag.

Zakahr sat for a moment, unable to believe she
knew—that that was all she had to say on the subject.
Conversation was not something Zakahr often pursued,
but despite the difficult subject matter, despite broach-
ing topics that were completely out of bounds, he was
enjoying her company. Except Lavinia was looking at
her watch.

'I really have to go home.'

'I'll take you now. I'll ring for my driver,' Zakahr
said, deciding it would be nice to see where she lived.
Only Lavinia wouldn't hear of it.

'I'm fine to drive.'

They walked through the streets, both in silence, back
towards the darkening offices.

'What did she say?' It was Zakahr who broke the
silence—curious despite himself. 'What did Nina say
when she found out I was her son?'

'She screamed—wailed.' Lavinia didn't soften the
brutal details of that day. 'It was one of the saddest
things I've ever seen.'

'She doesn't deserve sympathy.'

'She wasn't asking for it,' Lavinia said.

To Zakahr it felt strange to be talking about this. For so long it had been private knowledge. In the last few weeks it had come to the fore, with harsh words spoken with his so-called family, but now, like a cool breeze, Lavinia had swept into the most closed area of his life, and to be walking at eight p.m., to be talking about that which was never discussed, with a woman he had only just met, was as unfamiliar as it was refreshing.

She challenged him—made him question his own thoughts…duplicated them on occasion.

'Maybe you should hear what she has to say.' She was gentle rather than probing, but it touched the rawest of nerves.

'There's nothing to talk about with her—you yourself cut ties with your own mother.'

'No,' Lavinia corrected. 'I simply gave up trying to change her.'

Zakahr didn't want to think about it. Zakahr, as they reached the staff car park, wanted instead the easy solution.

Lavinia was incredibly pretty.

Her mouth, devoid of lipstick, was full and plump, and despite a few hours' sleep in the office still her body seeped with exhaustion. He thought how nice it would be to take her back to his hotel.

How much nicer for her, Zakahr thought, rather than driving home, to come back to his luxurious suite, to be pampered.

Sex, for Zakahr, was the equivalent of benzodiazepine.

It helped one sleep, and when the bottle ran out it was easily replaced. He had no qualms about one-night stands, one-week stands.… He caught a waft of her fragrance. Maybe, he realised, here was a woman who could hold his interest for a month.

'Thank you.' She smiled up at him as they reached her car. 'It's been really nice to talk.'

'We can talk some more.'

There was an invitation there, and Lavinia's body reacted to it—whether it was embarrassment at sleeping the afternoon away, or just that it had been so pleasant to actually talk about her problems, for a while there her guard had been down and she'd simply enjoyed his company. But there was a knot in her stomach as she faced him. Not the knot of anxiety that was familiar these days, but a knot far lower in her body, which tightened as she stood there. Her mouth, which had chatted easily all evening, felt now as if it were made of rubber as she tried to ignore his thinly veiled offer.

'I need my bed!' Lavinia said, then corrected herself. 'Bath and *then* bed!'

Zakahr was about to agree—in fact that was exactly what he had in mind—but he knew women, knew how to be subtle, knew exactly what he was doing… He lowered his head. A slow, soft kiss, a teasing taste, and then bath and bed would be arranged—except at his hotel.

Only Lavinia had other ideas.

It took a second to register her lips on his cheek, the feel of that plump mouth on his skin, saying goodbye as she might to any friend—a fleeting exchange after a pleasant evening.

'Thanks again.' Lavinia climbed into her car, hid her blush with her hair as she leant forward and put the key in the ignition. 'I'll see you in the morning. Have a good night.'

Lavinia drove out of the car park on autopilot, put in her card and willed the boom gate to rise, willed herself not to look in the rearview mirror, fighting a sudden urge to screech the car into reverse. So badly she wanted to go to him. She had felt rather than heard his invitation, and even if her mind had said no her body had felt more than inclined to accept.

How?

Lavinia turned into the city street and met a red traffic light. Now she looked in the rearview mirror, seeing not herself but her image—the woman Zakahr thought he saw.

What would he think if he knew the truth? That this outwardly assured, flirty woman had no experience with men—that even his casual kiss would be her first?

Lavinia was an extremely skilled flirt.

Her mother had taught her well, and now it happened without thought.

She could beckon a man to bed with one eye and warn him off with the other. It wasn't a case of being manipulative—for a while it had meant survival. And survival had been necessary for a teenager in some of the sleazier jobs Fleur had encouraged for her daughter.

Now twenty-four, and working for Kolovsky, she still retained those skills, but they were used more subtly. Of course she'd flirted with her bosses. But, rather as with the stunning garments they produced, she'd simply admired them, enjoyed them, loved to have a little play with them and dress up. Despite the rumours to the contrary, it had all been strictly fun.

Flirting with Zakahr, however innocent, was proving downright dangerous—like teasing a tiger behind bars. Here was one man Lavinia wasn't sure she could handle if he suddenly got out—and it was a relief to be away from him.

As she drove off, there was also relief for Zakahr. Normally he had no compunction about getting involved with staff, none at all—even his regular PA Abigail was an occasional lover—but he was here in Australia with the intention *not* to get involved. And certainly not with someone like Lavinia, who not only knew his past but was dealing with Rachael.

It had killed him to sit and listen to that—he didn't want to go through it again.

Zakahr poured vast amounts of money into helping damaged children—each company he resurrected was always structured to work closely with a charity. It came with unexpected benefits—staff were more eager, it promoted a sense of purpose. Yes, Zakahr walked the talk, but despite his great work there was no contact. He had left that part of his past behind, and never wanted to visit it again. Despite his impassiveness, hearing Lavinia speak of Rachael had swirled the black river of hate that ran through him.

No, Lavinia and her problems he did *not* need.

There was a lipgloss rolling around on the floor of the car. He kicked it under the seat opposite, but a moment or so later it rolled out again to him. He cursed, and picked it up and put it in his pocket.

The car slid past the casino, but that wasn't the sort of high Zakahr needed tonight.

He walked into the hotel and, instead of heading to his suite, headed to the plush bar—because he *did* need a good night.

He ordered a brandy, then saw a pretty face and jewels and lipstick and a smile across the room, hoping he might return it.

It was that easy for him.

But, no, Zakahr did *not* have the good night Lavinia had wished him. Because he pulled out a lipgloss instead of his pen when he went to sign for champagne, and, wondering if she'd hexed him, Zakahr downed his brandy in one and to the smile's disappointment headed up to his suite.

He took off his jacket. It smelt of her.

He took off his shirt, because that now smelt of her too.

He poured another brandy. The room's flowers had been replaced—an arrangement of lilies—and Zakahr felt a soft, thick petal. It felt like Lavinia's skin surely must… He stopped himself. He did not need names to faces.

Less than a week into his month, his decision was made. The House of Kolovsky would be no more—now all he had to do was execute it.

She'd get another job, he told himself. Yet his gut churned with sudden unease.

Zakahr headed to the bathroom, ran the tap and

splashed his face with water. As he reached for a towel he caught sight of his back in the angled mirrors—scars like tattoos all told their tale, and Zakahr had lived through each hellish one.

Rarely did Zakahr examine them, but he did now.

He saw the thick knot of flesh over his scapula, the dark purple circles that like the memories did not fade, and he was sixteen again, surviving the brutal streets—streetwise and hardened, but as scared as hell.

Here was the bigger picture, Zakahr told himself. *This* the reason he was here and he mustn't forget it.

Couldn't forget it.

God knew he'd tried.

CHAPTER SIX

'You need to sign this.' He did not look up as she handed him a document. He took a long drink of his coffee to escape the scent of her. 'Contracts are screaming for it—Aleksi should have done it before he left.'

'I'll read through it later.'

'They need it now.'

If they didn't she wouldn't be standing in his office. She was doing her best to avoid him, tapping away on the computer, seemingly engrossed in her work. But Contracts had demanded his signature, and like it or not Lavinia had to face the man who'd filled her thoughts all night, trying to pretend she wasn't the least concerned that tonight they were going out for dinner—and it wasn't dining with royalty that was daunting Lavinia.

'Rula is to be the new Face of Kolovsky—they're shooting this week, and her contract still hasn't been signed off.' Still he made no move. 'It's an important document.'

'Then it deserves close attention,' Zakahr retorted. 'Which I don't have time for now.'

'So what do I tell them?'

'That's entirely up to you.' He took another drink of his coffee. 'Out.'

He was loathsome, Lavinia decided as she hung up the phone after not the easiest of conversations with Contracts. He was loathsome, horrible and arrogant, and she was mad to even consider fancying him. In fact she refused to—so she checked her horoscope instead.

The stars are urging you to take the advice being given…

Fat lot of help that was—some advice on pompous, tall, dark and handsome bosses would be nice.

'Lavinia.'

With a jolt she looked up, and for a second was confused. But Iosef always did that to her, given he was Aleksi's identical twin. Though he had plenty of the Kolovsky dash, he was a smudge more down-to-earth than Aleksi, who wore only the best suits and had his hair trimmed weekly.

Iosef was in black jeans and a T-shirt, and didn't look in the best of moods.

'Is he in?'

'He is!' Lavinia smiled up at Iosef—he had always been her favourite of the Kolovsky brothers, and they'd shared a little flirtation in the past—well, till he'd fallen head-over-heels and married Annie.

'How is it going?'

Lavinia rolled her eyes.

'What are you doing at this desk?'

'I'm the new PA!'

Iosef actually laughed, and for a moment so too did Lavinia.

'What's he like to work for?'

'He makes the rest of you look positively docile. I'll just let him know that you're here.'

'No need.' Zakahr was at the door, his expression boot-faced. 'Carry on surfing the net, Lavinia.'

Zakahr closed the door. Iosef was already sitting down, and Zakahr was rattled that he hadn't waited to be asked, at his clear familiarity with the place.

With Lavinia.

For now he pushed that from his mind.

'How are things?' Iosef asked, not remotely embarrassed at being overheard. Arrogance was a strong genetic trait. 'How are you finding it?'

Zakahr did not answer.

'How's Lavinia doing as PA?'

'Are you here to make small talk?' Zakahr could not be bothered with small talk.

'I have just come from visiting our mother.'

'*Your* mother,' Zakahr corrected. 'Her choice,' he added, because from the day she and his father had abandoned a newborn baby in Detsky Dom she had no longer been his.

'I spoke at length with her psychiatrist yesterday. She is in a fragile mental state.' Like Zakahr, Iosef did not mince words. He did not want to be here—he understood completely his brother's take—but always with family there was a strange sense of duty. 'I was not going to come to you with this, but I've spoken with my wife and we now agree you should at least be told. What you do with the information is up to you. Nina wants to meet with you, to speak with you…'

'And then it will all be okay?' Zakahr sneered. 'I would check this psychiatrist's qualifications—because if she is in such a fragile state does he *really* want me to say all I have to? All I want to? Does he think I am going to walk in and forgive her?'

'He has warned her how damaging this confrontation could be for her at this stage of her treatment—but still she is desperate to see you.'

'Tell her it's too late,' Zakahr said. 'Thirty-six years too late.'

Iosef nodded and stood to leave. He had not come here to argue or to plead, and he had known this would be difficult—that Zakahr wanted nothing to do with them.

When he got to the door he changed his mind. 'Annie and I are having Annika and Ross over on Saturday for dinner. It would be good to see you…' Iosef hesitated. He knew so little about this man who was his brother, and was trying hard to do the right thing. They actually *weren't* having Annika and Ross over, but if Zakahr would only agree he knew his sister and her husband would come. 'If you want to bring anyone…'

'You still don't get it.' Zakahr leant back in his chair. 'I am not here for a tender reunion with my *family*.' His lips sneered the word. 'Aleksi I have respect for. The rest of you…'

'We didn't know.'

'You didn't *want* to know,' Zakahr said, but Iosef shook his head.

'We are all devastated by this, Riminic…' And Iosef could have kicked himself. He had spent the morning hearing his mother wailing and crying the name of the baby she had abandoned, and now he stood before the man who loathed his past so much he had wiped it clean and changed his name. 'Zakahr…'

'Get out.' Zakahr did not shout it, but it was non-negotiable. Just hearing the name Riminic made the bile churn in his stomach.

Riminic Ivan Kolovsky.

Riminic, son of Ivan.

He could feel the sweat on his forehead as the name played over and over. All Riminic had done, all Riminic had endured.

He never wanted to hear that name again.

Nina could die screaming it, but *he* never wanted to hear it.

Riminic was gone, Ivan was gone, and if he had his way so too would be the House of Kolovksy.

'Zakahr!' Lavinia's voice came over the intercom and he pressed his fingers together and to his lips. The light breeze of her voice hauled him from the eye of the storm. 'I need to pop out for an hour.'

'Another appointment?'

'Actually, yes.' She hesitated before continuing, 'Then I've got to get my hair done, and I'm meeting Katina back here at five to sort out my outfit for tonight…'

'Your point is…?'

'I won't be back this afternoon. You'll have to manage without me.'

There was the crackle of the intercom, an unseen

blush, a call to flirt, an inappropriate response there for the taking. She willed him not to, and thankfully Zakahr obliged.

'Fine.'

'How?' Ms Hewitt asked for the twentieth time, and the answer was, as always, impossible.

In an effort to look more presentable on paper, Lavinia had officially promoted herself to PA, but Ms Hewitt was now questioning how she could hold down such a responsible job *and* be a full-time carer for Rachael.

'I'm sure I won't be the first single working mum.'

'Rachael will need a lot of attention,' Ms Hewitt said.

'Then I'll go part-time,' Lavinia said. But even that didn't appease the case worker. Not that anything Lavinia could say was going to convince Ms Hewitt that Lavinia was a responsible adult—she still saw Lavinia as the angry, troubled girl she had been all those years ago.

'Have you really thought this through at all, Lavinia?'

'I've thought of nothing else,' Lavinia said.

This whole hour had been pointless. Now the clock was edging towards four. She had her hair appointment soon, then the dinner to get ready for—not that she could tell Ms Hewitt *that*.

'How long till you reach your decision?'

'Lavinia, it's not a cut and dried decision. We're about keeping families together, not pulling them apart.'

'I *am* her family,' Lavinia attempted again, but it

fell on deaf ears. 'Can I at least see her—it's nearly a week now!'

'You can see her tomorrow afternoon for an hour—but, Lavinia, Rachael needs calm. She doesn't need to know that the adults in her life are fighting over her. When you see her, just keep things light.'

'I can't tell her I want her?'

'Her father *wants* her.' Ms Hewitt's words were abrupt. 'She has a family that wants her. Yes, it's a family that might need extended support…' Lavinia opened her mouth to argue, but Ms Hewitt overrode her. 'But making false promises to Rachael isn't going to help matters. Try to keep things even.'

God, why was *she* being made to feel like the bad guy?

It took every ounce of will-power to stay calm and thank Ms Hewitt, but as Lavinia sat at the hairdresser's she was shaking with silent rage as her thick blonde hair was curled into spirals and pinned.

'Problem?' Zakahr checked as she stomped back into the office after her appointment.

'Only of my own making!'

Oh, she'd sworn her distance from him, but Zakahr was *there*, just at the right moment, and asking a question. It was like a champagne cork popping. Her rage was fizzing out, years and years of rage spluttering over the edges with such ferocity Lavinia's eyes actually stung with tears.

'She'll send her back to Kevin,' Lavinia said.

'You don't know that.' Zakahr wished he hadn't asked the question—wished he hadn't heard Lavinia's response. He gave his brief, soothing answer and turned to go.

'She sent *me* back to my mother time after time.' Lavinia's words hit his turning back like arrows. 'I'm supposed to keep things *even* with Rachael and not make promises I can't keep. I'm not even supposed to tell her I want to raise her.'

'*Can* you raise her?' Zakahr challenged—because he believed in action rather than words, and before he offered his support where a child was concerned he had to be sure. 'Or is this just a cause for now?'

'It's why I bought a house—I've got a room for her at home that I'm waiting to decorate. I've wanted Rachael in my care since she was born. But I'm not supposed to confuse her with all that.' She shook her head, cross with herself for bringing her problems to work, for exploding in front of him. 'Just leave it.' She brushed past him, heading for the safety of her office.

'Ms Hewitt is wrong.' Zakahr halted her. 'All this stuff about keeping your distance, not building up her hopes.' He could see Lavinia do a double-take, could see her try to speak, to tell him this was not his concern— except right now it was. 'Take her to your home, show her the room, tell her that no matter what happens, what is decided, it is always there for her. Say that you will do your very best to get her there—that even if you are not able to look after her now you are thinking of her, and that the room is *hers*, waiting.'

'Go against everything I've been told?' Lavinia's knuckles were white on the office door. 'I could lose her.'

'You're losing her every day you are not honest,'

Zakahr insisted. 'How many milkshakes, how many dolls, how many clothes will fill her soul? She needs to know that you love her, and that you are doing every-thing you can for her—even if she can't see it, even if it doesn't feel like it.'

'Build up her hopes?' Lavinia challenged. 'And then what if she finds out she's going back…?'

'She might not,' Zakahr said. 'And if she does…' he was exasperated because it was surely simple '…buy her a phone.'

'She's not even five!'

'A cheap phone.'

'She'll lose it. They'll take it off her.'

'Then buy her another—and another,' Zakahr said. 'You can text her a kiss each night.'

'Ms Hewitt said—'

'Are you going to change your mind?' Zakahr demanded.

'Of course not.'

'Because *that* is Ms Hewitt's concern. I can guarantee it. That Rachael will be too much like hard work—that Mr Right will come along but he won't want children, or not someone else's. *Are* you going to change your mind?'

'No.'

'Then let them accuse you of loving her too much. So long as it doesn't wane, their argument won't last.'

'I don't know…' Lavinia admitted. But when he said it like that, it made sense. 'I want to tell her, but…' She shook her head. 'I need to think.'

'You need a lawyer…' Zakahr said.

'I need a drink,' Lavinia corrected, pulling the ring on an energy drink as Katina waltzed in with an armful of gowns. 'And to get ready.' She gave him a thin smile. 'Thank you for listening.'

Zakahr shook his head. 'I wish *you* would listen.'

CHAPTER SEVEN

'No.' KATINA was definite. 'It's not your colour.'

'It's stunning,' Lavinia begged—because the dress *was* heavenly, and more importantly they had not a moment to spare.

But Katina would not budge.

'You represent Kolovsky. You're dining with a king. I choose.' Katina pulled down the zipper and Lavinia wriggled out. Katina bundled up the peach dress with a warning to Lavinia to do her make-up as she left her standing in her panties and bra. 'You're running very late.'

She *would* have put on her war paint—except her make-up bag was at her desk.

Had it been Aleksi, or even Levander, she'd have just padded out there—not caring if they were there or not. She'd even have answered the phone had it been ringing. The brothers were so used to it they wouldn't notice. But Zakahr came from the staid world of finance.

With Zakahr—Lavinia swallowed—it was different. Very different indeed.

'Would you mind fetching me my bag?' She settled for popping her head around the door and calling out to him. But Zakahr was in his own office, and he could not believe her gall.

He walked out to tell her so—and there was her skinny shoulder and her clavicle, and the deep red silk strap of a bra. He *got* that this was normal around here— he had been down to the design rooms and the dressing rooms and had seen far more than a shoulder—and he was also exceptionally used to women in their natural form in his own personal life.

'It's in the second drawer,' Lavinia directed.

He practically threw it at her.

'Thank you.'

'You could have waited till you were dressed and got it yourself,' he said tartly.

'And spilled foundation on a Kolovsky creation? I don't think so,' Lavinia called back. But despite her quick comeback she was blushing right down to her toes, and she leant her head on the door for a moment as she closed it.

Why did he have to go and be nice about Rachael? Why couldn't he have ignored her, as he had all morning? How, *how*, was she supposed to get through tonight?

It was too dangerous to ponder, so she drained her energy drink and then slapped on some foundation, rouged a cleavage where there was none, and painted her face with more than her usual care. By then Katina had returned. Lavinia frowned at the rather bold colours, but she held up her arms as the dress slithered down her skin, delighting in the rich caress of the silk. And, yes, when she stepped back and looked in the mirror Lavinia accepted that Katina had been right!

'It's perfect,' Lavinia breathed, craning her neck for a view from behind as Katina strapped her into the highest of heels. 'I'd never have chosen these colours.'

'I told you…' Katina said, and she stepped back, scrutinising Lavinia carefully. And she was never one to lavish compliments—at least not with the staff. 'I wasn't sure you could carry it off.' She handed her a sheer golden net overcoat, and before she left warned Lavinia she had to sign it in when she brought it back in the morning.

'But for now you're all mine!' Lavinia grinned at the mirror.

Her hair had been curled into long thick blonde ringlets, and loosely piled on top of her head, and her eyes were bluer than ever, thanks to lashings of mascara. But her lipstick was neutral, and she added one final layer of gloss before stepping out to where Zakahr stood, fiddling with his tie at a full-length mirror, reeking of expensive cologne and, on reflection, looking thoroughly fed-up.

Until he caught her eyes in the mirror.

She saw him blink as he slowly turned around.

'You look amazing!' He couldn't *not* say it—there was no disputing the fact; Zakahr felt his tongue on the roof of his mouth as she teetered towards the mirror in a blaze of gold and red and orange.

'I know!' She gave him a wide grin, and it was so unlike any of the usual responses to a compliment he almost smiled. Then she handed him a tie and jiggled with the dress, rearranging very small breasts into some sort of cleavage. 'I know I didn't want the job, but I love the perks!'

'Kolovsky silk?'

'Of course,' Lavinia said. 'As is this tie.' She handed him Katina's choice, but Zakahr stared at it in disgust. 'It would choke me,' Zakahr said, and then corrected himself. 'I choose my own ties.'

'Not when you're accompanying me!' Lavinia said. 'Put it on.'

And, given he now ran the place, he supposed he must.

It was grey, but there were flecks of a colour there from beyond the spectrum, and a silvery tinge that turned his suit into evening wear.

'You know,' Lavinia twittered on, 'Kolovsky silk changes depending on the wearer's mood.'

'Rubbish.'

'That tie was a midnight-blue. I swear it.' Lavinia blinked at the transformation. 'Now it's cold and grey.' She gave him a sweet smile. 'It matches your eyes.'

He couldn't help but stare at her. The dress shimmered gold, and there were flashes of red that moved as she did, dancing like an aura around her body.

'I'd better not spill anything. Katina will never forgive me!'

'You don't get to keep it?'

'God, no!' Lavinia said. 'It's just on loan for the night—like me!' She picked up his wrist and glanced at his watch. 'You've got me till eleven.'

Eleven a.m., preferably, Zakahr thought. Because when she was close all he wanted was to kiss her. He could feel her thin fingers around his wrist, smell her fragrant hair and see the fiery reds darting across the heavy silk, shimmering and then darkening. It was as if it blushed around her breasts, the curve of her waist. Her skin was pale, and there was a lot on display, long limbed and slender. He wanted to lower his head and brand her skin. He wanted now the pleasure that must surely be his soon. She was, Zakahr decided, if she'd only stay quiet, completely gorgeous.

'Should you cover yourself…?' Zakahr started, but Lavinia knew those rules at least.

Words like *pashmina* and *wrap* and *shrug* were not in Zakahr's vocabulary. He watched as she pulled on the golden net, covering her arms, skimming down to mid-calf. She looked like a captured mermaid, and he wanted to tear off the net, to free her, to say to hell with Kolovsky and the dignitaries downstairs, to lay her on the office floor and take her now.

'Come on, then.' She seemed completely oblivious to the charged air. She just clipped ahead of him in heels that were impossibly high, squirting perfume as they walked and informing him that an exclusive restaurant had been booked, and was one that they used regularly—the rear closed off for their guests. It was an extremely upmarket vegetarian restaurant, where Aleksi usually took his guests—which saved any cultural awkwardness.

'I'd kill for a steak,' Zakahr said, and sighed.

'And no alcohol,' Lavinia warned.

'Lavinia.' They were in the lift. 'I *have* done this before.'

'You nearly didn't go to the airport,' Lavinia pointed out.

It was morning in Europe, so the car-ride was taken

up with Zakahr firing off e-mails on his phone. Already her feet were killing her, but Lavinia distracted herself by chatting to Eddie and annoying Zakahr as she did so.

'I'm working,' Zakahr snapped as her laughter sailed through the car.

'We're *all* working!' Lavinia pointed out, winking at Eddie as she did so. 'Just some of us manage to smile as we do so.'

She wasn't so assured a moment later.

'The press are here.' Lavinia swallowed as they approached. 'The restaurant's usually discreet. How would the press have found…?'

But quickly Lavinia realized, as she stepped out of the car, that it wasn't the royals who awaited them that had captured the nation's interest. It was the man who walked beside her.

'Oh, God…' Absolutely Lavinia wasn't prepared for this—she was used to cameras in a more controlled setting—and the unexpected frenzy that circled them had her spinning momentarily, wondering if she should have foreseen this, if there was a detail she had overlooked in tonight's preparation.

'Just walk.' He sounded completely at ease, and he made it sound easy—except her legs wouldn't obey his simple command. Then, perhaps realising she was struggling, he offered assistance, put his arm loosely around her, to guide her.

But as his hand touched her waist the contact almost shot Lavinia into the throng of photographers. She could feel his hand on her waist more than she could feel her sore feet!

'Come on.' It was twenty-four steps to the restaurant. Lavinia knew because each one took effort. She could smell him, she could feel him, but more than that he was aware of her too.

She knew that.

Knew because when they entered the restaurant it was just herself and Zakahr—their guests hadn't arrived—and it daunted her. The conversation that had flowed so easily was horribly awkward now.

'They should be here soon.' Lavinia flashed a smile at a passing waiter, just for something to do. 'Could I have champagne, please?' But even as she said it she remembered her own warning. 'Actually, make that a Diet Co…' Her voice trailed off, because that didn't actually go with the dress. 'Just a sparkling water, please.' She sighed and rolled her eyes. 'Lucky me!'

And then she looked across the table and saw him smiling—not grinning, just looking at her and smiling, his dark lips suddenly dangerous, those cold grey eyes warming. And it was attraction—pure, naked attraction—in surely its most potent form. And for the first time in her life she was sampling it.

She sat there as his eyes roamed her.

She breathed in, and then she breathed out, and then she couldn't remember how to any more.

She could feel a pulse in the side of her neck. She knew his eyes were upon it, and she wanted it to be his mouth.

'I'll get you champagne later,' Zakahr said, and for

the first time with a man Lavinia felt the floor slip beneath her, felt the frantic dash of her feet to find solid ground. Because for the first time with a man Lavinia felt suddenly out of her depth.

'I'll stick with water,' she said. 'It's far safer.'

Thankfully their guests arrived, and Lavinia was more than a little relieved when, after she rose to greet them, the King's aides subtly moved her further down the table. The men and women were sitting separately, which meant that, without the distraction of Zakahr, Lavinia could concentrate on the Princess.

Unlike the Queen, Princess Jasmine was veiled, as was the tradition for unmarried women of their small, prosperous land.

'The women of today know what they want.' The Queen smiled in the direction of her daughter. 'Jasmine knows exactly the dress she wants—though it is hard to capture that along with all our traditions. Throughout the marriage service slowly she will be revealed. Then we have the problem that some of her maids are married, others are betrothed, some from different lands...' The Queen shook her head in exasperation. 'Kolovsky is the only Western designer we could trust to fulfil all our wishes.'

'Oh, they will,' Lavinia said assuredly, then turned her attention to Jasmine, her interest completely genuine. 'So what sort of dress *do* you want?' she asked. 'I can't wait to see what the designers come up with.'

His so-called brothers had overlooked a rare asset, Zakahr realised as he worked through dinner. It could have been the most awkward of dinners. Jasmine, out in public, was veiled, and Lavinia ate like a bird, so food was hardly top of either woman's agenda, but it was the conversation and laughter that flowed.

Yes, Lavinia spoke just a little *too* much, and once he noticed she actually interrupted the Queen, but—used to entertaining, and all too aware of its pitfalls—Zakahr, on a professional level, found it was actually a relief to have Lavinia with him. King Abdullah required close attention—the King was extremely clever, and he wanted to speak business, which Zakahr did best—and it was made easier knowing the rest of the guests were being attended to. After all, was there anyone on this earth who could talk weddings like Lavinia?

Zakahr doubted it.

Not once, he noted, did her eyes glaze over as the Princess described the Kolovsky designers' visions for her and the bridal party. In fact Lavinia kept halting the Princess and asking for more detail, which the Princess and her mother were only too happy to provide.

'My daughter is enjoying herself.' As the Princess and her mother's laughter filled the table the King followed Zakahr's gaze. 'Lavinia is charming.'

She certainly was. Zakahr's eyes lingered, and perhaps she felt them, because suddenly she looked up and she met his gaze—only she didn't smile and look away.

Lavinia could hear the glasses chinking, the laughter, the noise of the restaurant, but all she could see was this beautiful man as his eyes caressed her from across the crowded table. There was heat in her cheeks, and she was trapped by his stare, dizzy at her own thought-processes. Startled, she finally pulled her eyes away, tried to concentrate on the conversation, but her mind was still with Zakahr.

The restaurant was warm, and maybe the difficult week was catching up with her, Lavinia told herself as her temples pounded to the beat of her own pulse.

She took a sliver of dragon fruit, felt the cool fruit on her tongue, but it didn't cool her head.

'Excuse me.' She headed for the opulent ladies' room, turned the heavy gold taps and ran water over her wrists. Then she sat on the lounger.

Lavinia pressed her fingers into her eyes as something close to panic washed over her.

Piece by piece, Zakahr had dismantled her armoury.

She could deal with men—any man, Lavinia told herself.

She was *trained* to keep men at a distance.

Except so easily he disarmed her.

She took a couple of slow deep breaths, told herself she could deal with it, and then removed her hands from her eyes and stood. There was a huge gold mirror, and Lavinia looked at her sleek reflection, looked at the dress and the jewels on loan, and the ringlets that were starting to loosen, and she wanted to be *her*, Lavinia thought. She actually wanted to step into the mirror and escape.

Wanted to give in to the beat of her body, to be the woman of the world Zakahr thought she was…

'Everything okay?' Zakahr checked as she walked past.

Coffees had been served; the table was relaxed.

Jasmine had moved seats and was now speaking with her father.

'Of course. It's been a good night.'

It *had* been a good night—so much so, the King did not wait for the end of the meal to extend his own invitation.

'We would love to have you as our guests before we return to our land—I will have my aide contact you.' He shook hands with Zakahr. 'It has been worth the trip—though I was sceptical,' the King admitted. 'I wanted to use our own designers—I did not see why we had to come to you. Usually it is the other way round.'

Out of the restaurant and out of the noise, exhaustion hit Lavinia. She was so tired she was dizzy—as if she'd drunk a whole bottle of champagne—and her feet were positively killing her.

"Where's Eddie?' Unlike Zakahr, Lavinia noticed that their car had a different driver.

'He got called away.' This driver was far more polished than Eddie, and politely rebuffed Lavinia's further questioning. Zakahr Belenki was the man to impress and, partition closed, the car slid through the night.

Zakahr sat opposite her. He watched as she unstrapped her shoes, and there was a moan of bliss and a look of rapture on her face as she peeled them off—both Zakahr wanted to revisit later, and he was quietly confident that he would.

'Where are we going?' Lavinia frowned at the unfamiliar direction.

'I told you there would be champagne.'

'No champagne for me!' Lavinia snapped a smile.

'I have to drive home.' She didn't bother with the partition, just pressed the intercom and gave the driver her instructions

The car pulled in at the large multi-storey car park, where the staff parked their cars—except it was closed for the night, and cars could only exit now. The driver was clearly a little torn between leaving Lavinia to walk alone through the concrete jungle or having his esteemed passenger sit and wait. 'Would you mind waiting, sir,' he asked Zakahr, 'while I escort Lavinia…?'

'I'll walk her,' Zakahr said, quite sure they'd soon be returning.

Lavinia didn't usually *do* shy—she was used to beautiful people, used to working alongside strong, male energy, and had survived at Kolovsky by *not* being overawed or intimidated—but she was shy as they walked through the concrete enclosure of the car park. She carried her shoes, but wished she'd put up with the pain and kept them on—because beside him she felt swamped.

'Thank you.' She turned and smiled at him when they reached her car, then looked in her bag for her keys.

Zakahr could see one heavy ringlet falling over her eye and had to bunch his fist in order not to move it. He could not read her, could not work her out—usually he did not have to, did not want to. The flirting game was a mere means to an end for Zakahr.

Lavinia, Zakahr knew, could prove tricky at work, but sometimes in her company he escaped the loop of revenge and hate. He had smiled, he had laughed, and it was she who made it happen. Zakahr wanted more.

'Are you sure you don't want that champagne?' Zakahr asked.

She was about to deliver her firm response, only her mind was at odds.

She wanted champagne.

She wanted his bed.

She wanted the woman in the mirror to step into passion.

She was, Lavinia thought, quite possibly going crazy.

'Lavinia?'

She heard her name but she didn't look up. She found her keys and stared at them. She heard the tip in his voice, heard his unvoiced question. Still she didn't look up, because so badly she wanted to say yes to him. His fingers took a lock of her hair as she stood there, and there was an urge to sink into him, to kiss the wrist she could see, to lean on to his chest, to have someone hold her up for a little while.

She was scared to look up, because her warning look was off. But she did it anyway. She looked up into lust and into the blissful escape of him.

She knew the danger, but so sweet would be the reward.

Lavinia turned the key.

One kiss goodnight, she insisted to herself.

He lowered his head slowly, wondered if her mouth would again meet his cheek, hoping that this time it would swell to his.

Only it didn't swell. Instead it rested against his lips.

Her forehead pressed to his, and her mouth did not move at first. It just slowly met his. Her first taste of him, and she savoured it. She felt the pulse of his lip, and she let herself feel it, and then his lips moved across hers, his kiss slow and measured and so skilled that for the recipient no experience was required. All she had to do was accept it, move with it, give in to it. And then she got the reward of his tongue—it was so cool and luxurious it was like drinking gold. There had been no teenage kisses for Lavinia—her youth had been spent warding off men—and now as a woman she tasted heaven.

Kissing bored Zakahr.

He had kissed many—so many; he started at this point only as a means to swiftly moving on. A means to an end because it was what women wanted.

Only *this* kiss he enjoyed. This kiss he chose to linger over. She tasted sweet, and her mouth was soft. He tasted deeper. His hands roamed her body—not to progress things, but to stay a rare while longer. He felt her waist, and then down to her bottom as his tongue stroked hers. She was gorgeous, but too slender, on the cusp of ripening, and Zakahr wanted to be there to witness it. He was imagining more curves to her body, in his arms a taste of potential that he wanted to explore, but he halted that strange thought-process because Zakahr didn't *do* futures. Zakahr lived for one night.

Now he could lift his head and without a word take her by the hand back to the luxury of his car—could kiss her again as they headed for his hotel. Except still he wanted to linger, wanted to kiss her some more, and Lavinia was happy to oblige.

The caress of his hands was exquisite. She could feel the heat on her skin, imagined him leaving a trail of red on gold, but with the taste of his lips there was room for no other thoughts. He was strong and male, but there was a glimpse of tenderness, a skill to his lips that taught and she followed, a danger to his kiss that took her to places she'd never intended to go.

The feel of his hands was sublime—his mouth a retreat from the hammer of her thoughts. Only now did she realise the panic of her existence. Because for the very first time her mind met with beautiful silence. There was just one thought to follow, one need, one want to succumb to, and instead of someone else's tonight the need was *hers*.

His hand moved to the padding of her bra, stroking her through the silk, but the dense material dimmed the pleasure. She kissed him—deeper she kissed him. She didn't want it to end, and neither did Zakahr. He almost breathed an apology when she removed his hand from her breast, but moaned into her mouth as he realised it wasn't modesty she was requesting in the deserted car park. Lavinia guided him to the zipper, and he slid it down just enough to slide his hand inside and free her.

She hated her non-existent breasts—should have been embarrassed that he first met with padding—but his quickening breathing spelt desire. His thumb met her nipple, his palm cupped her small breast, and she swelled in his hand. His fingers were stroking the tender flesh beneath her arms, and it was as if her thighs were too heavy for her legs. Her body whimpered for more, and Zakahr grew harder at her pleasure.

'Come with me…' He could not continue this here— would not. 'Come with me,' he said again, his mouth, his tongue working hard between the words. The pad of his thumb on her nipple and the heat in his groin were intense, and there was no relief as he pressed it into her.

No relief for Lavinia either.

She wanted to.

So cautious with men, tonight—with him—she didn't want to be cautious any more. She wanted to give in to the begging of her body and let him lead her away.

She wanted him to pick her up now and carry her to his car.

She wanted to fall on his million-thread-count sheets and be looked after.

She knew she could not.

Knew when his lips left hers the night must be over.

She could feel him pressed into her and she pushed back, felt his hand dig into her bottom as he pressed her in harder still. She didn't want this to end. Her kisses were frantic, and it was Zakahr who halted them.

'Come on.' He *had* to stop now. 'Come on.'

The world came crashing in.

Her world. She was supposed to be being responsible—not standing kissing in a car park at midnight, not pressed up to a man she had known less than a week.

'I can't.'

The statement was almost cruel. She could feel his hardness, knew her bold exploration of his body's reaction had brought them both close to the brink. And now she was changing her mind. Lavinia would have given *anything* for it to be otherwise.

She'd dropped her keys. Somewhere in this she'd dropped her keys and her handbag and her shoes. She sank to the floor to retrieve them, mortified because she knew she appeared nothing more than a tease.

'Don't play me, Lavinia…'

'I'm not,' she attempted—except she had. Lavinia knew that. She'd never had the intention to go back with him; had been a completely willing participant in a kiss that had got out of hand. She tried to keep her voice even. 'We have to work together…'

She'd worked with Aleksi, he almost pointed out. But he bit down on that caustic remark. Zakahr did not get her, was unsure as to the game she was playing, though quite sure that she *was* playing.

'I just don't think it's right that I go back to your hotel.'

'Why?' Zakahr asked, and then said, the barb on his tongue one he could not swallow down, 'Do you prefer car parks?'

CHAPTER EIGHT

IT WAS just a kiss. She almost convinced herself as she parked her car in her reserved space, burning with shame at what had taken place on this very spot.

He thought her cheap.

Lavinia knew that.

Thought her a tease and a flirt—*if only he knew the truth.*

Lavinia handed over the dress and signed the book, and then took the lift up to the office, bracing herself to face him—she would deal with this the only way she knew how.

Wearing a high ponytail, high heels, silver eyeshadow, and a silver top under a grey linen suit, she swished into the office a full twenty minutes early, bearing chocolate croissants and a smile that made people want to join her.

If Zakahr had been expecting awkwardness—her notice, even—he got neither.

'About last night…' As she placed his coffee and a pastry on his desk, Lavinia somehow managed to look him straight in the eye. 'I'd like to apologise for my behaviour.'

'*Our* behaviour,' Zakahr corrected. 'We were both there.'

'Well, I just want you to know that it was completely out of character for me.' She did her best not to notice the slight rise of one eyebrow. 'I've been running on too little sleep, and that combined with too many energy drinks yesterday…'

'I wasn't aware they were so potent.' He actually admired that she faced him head-on. 'Lavinia…'

Zakahr closed his eyes for just a moment. Really, he should just accept her apology at face value and move on. Soon he could move on—except she worried him so. He'd been here less than a week, the internal auditors were coming in… In three short weeks Lavinia would be out of a job, and somehow he had to warn her.

'Maybe I was hasty…' He had to word this so carefully—could not let her even glimpse the real meaning behind his words. 'When I insisted you became my PA I did not realise you had so much to contend with.' He watched her rapid blink. 'I don't want a PA who has to survive on energy drinks…'

'I slept well last night.'

Lucky for her, Zakahr thought. Because every time *he* had closed his eyes their kiss had replayed.

'Next week will be different. I'm seeing Rachael this afternoon—'

'Lavinia,' Zakahr broke in. 'I need someone who can work sixty-hour weeks—who can drop everything and do as the job demands.'

'Are you firing me?'

'Of course not.' Zakahr wished that sometimes she

wasn't so direct. 'All I'm suggesting is that, given your situation, maybe you should start thinking of a job that has more child-friendly hours.'

'Such as?' Those bright eyes flashed a shade darker, and Zakahr had no answer. 'With all *my* dazzling qualifications…?'

'I could give you a glowing reference.'

'Saying what?' Lavinia challenged. 'Lavinia's computer skills are excellent? She checks her e-mails hourly…?'

'You're good at your job.' Zakahr was aware of her lack of formal qualifications, and uncomfortably aware that another job that paid like Kolovsky would not be easy for Lavinia to come by. 'You're personable, you're good with clients…'

'And I love my old job,' Lavinia finished for him. 'Once you've hired a PA I can go back to it.'

He couldn't help her without revealing the truth. He had tried, Zakahr told himself—her future was not his responsibility.

'Fine,' Zakahr clipped, and glanced at his watch. 'I have to go down to Design.'

It was an unusual situation for Zakahr. Usually he was openly assessing a company—closing it or salvaging it. Once it was acquired by Belenki he hand-picked staff to ensure its smooth running, but here at Kolovsky, in order to maintain the façade before pulling the pin, the day-to-day running he was usually too busy for was up to him.

He sat through the most mind-numbingly boring visual of the first images for Princess Jasmine's wedding dress.

He had absolutely no *passion* for the product, as Lavinia would say, but he did his best to hide it and congratulated the designers. Cross-eyed with boredom, he headed out—just in time to catch Lavinia lounging against the wall and talking into her phone. But she was clearly waiting for him, because she turned it off when she saw Zakahr approached.

'You need to approve some shots and sign that contract.'

Zakahr rolled his eyes.

'Urgently,' Lavinia added, handing him a large folder. 'It's the new range,' she explained. 'We have to get these out today.'

'Are you going back to the office?'

Lavinia shook her head. 'It's almost lunchtime.'

'So soon?'

'It's almost one.' She completely missed his sarcasm and drifted back to her topic as Zakahr flicked through the folder. 'Just sign them and I'll drop them off. I shan't be around this afternoon—I've got to go down and have Katina sort out an evening wardrobe for me.' Lavinia gave a delighted grin. 'I'm starting to love my new job!'

He was about to ask how, given she was so rarely there, but Zakahr was fast realising sarcasm was wasted on her. If anything, it made her laugh. Lavinia was the oddest person he had ever met—utterly beautiful, but stunningly direct.

'Gorgeous, isn't she?' Lavinia commented, peering over his shoulder.

Zakahr wasn't so sure. Rula certainly *could* be

gorgeous, with her tumble of auburn hair and cool green eyes, yet she was beyond thin. Even the thick Kolovsky silk she was draped in did nothing to add a curve, and the underwear shots were to Zakahr unappealing.

'She's so thin.'

'I know.' There was almost a sigh of envy from Lavinia, but she rolled her eyes at herself. 'God, I am *so* glad to be out of that game.'

'What game?'

She put two fingers to her mouth. 'I couldn't do it,' she admitted.

'Too squeamish?'

'Too hungry!' Lavinia corrected.

'This is what Nina would have had you aim for?'

Lavinia just shrugged. 'It wasn't for me.'

'I'll have a look through these and get them back this afternoon.'

'Are you sure?' Lavinia checked. 'In that case I've got ten minutes.' She stopped at a door. 'I'm just going to have a quick peek. Are you coming?'

'Sorry?'

'The fabric Princess Jasmine has chosen?'

'I've just sat through a half-hour presentation.' Zakahr's head actually ached because he'd been so bored. It bemused him that she expected him to be keen, that they all were so devoted to *material*! 'I've seen the images, the swatches…'

'It's not the same.' Lavinia pushed open the door and they stepped inside a vast room, with shelf after shelf filled with rolls of fabric. The fabric codes were all in a computer, and an assistant located them and brought the rolls to a desk, where they were laid side by side. As she ran her hand over them finally Lavinia could properly picture it.

Zakahr, not for the first time, stood bored, hard-pushed to feign even mild interest—where was a financial crisis when he needed one?

'Thank you.' Lavinia, satisfied now that she could actually speak with the Princess about her choices, went to walk out. But suddenly she changed her mind, pressing in an access code, pushing on a heavy door and beckoning him in. 'Here.'

She gestured down a long aisle of fabric, and then down another one, through a maze of silk. Zakahr followed the blaze of silver ahead, with ponytail swinging, past endless corridors of colour till Lavinia stopped.

'This is my absolute favourite.'

Zakahr stared nonplussed at the neutral fabric, watched as she pressed a button till a metre or two of the silk had rippled down. Lavinia ran it through her fingers.

'Isn't it beautiful?' Lavinia said, and then she paused. She had been about to say *your father*, but she knew how that irked him, so without missing a beat Lavinia used his name. 'Ivan spent months getting this right—this is one of the original fabrics that made Kolovsky so famous.'

'It's beige.'

'No.' She held her hand up to it. 'It's more a cream—and look…' she slipped her hand behind it '…now it's pink. The fabric is called *koža*.'

'That means skin.' He was a little bit curious now. He

held it between his fingers, watched as the pinks faded to more golden hues, and it actually *felt* like skin—cool skin. He could see her hand stroking the fabric, see it running through her long fingers, and for the first time Zakahr realised that material could be beautiful—so beautiful. He prolonged the contact as he asked himself how it could be that a piece of material could be erotic.

How could simple, neutral cloth provoke reaction?

But, watching her hand stroke the fabric, watching her fingers while feeling the *koža* beneath his, he actually felt as if she were touching him.

'It's divine, isn't it?' Lavinia breathed. 'Normally they use this as a slip dress. It couldn't actually *be* a dress— you'd look as if you had nothing…' Her voice petered out as she watched his strong hand run beneath the cloth, saw the ripples it made as if she was wearing the fabric he held, as if it were her skin beneath his fingers, as if he were stroking her…

'Why?' Zakahr asked in a voice that wasn't quite as steady as he'd like. 'Why do you say these things?'

'I don't!' Lavinia said, and she was cringing. 'Whatever I say around you…' She couldn't explain it. It was like innuendo city—every road led there!

'What do you want, Lavinia?' Zakahr already knew what *he* wanted, but she had to want something—of that he was sure.

'I don't know,' Lavinia admitted. She wanted his kiss, she wanted everything they had almost had, but she was quite sure—positive, in fact—that if he knew her truth he wouldn't want her. 'I'm trying not to think about you.'

'Maybe stop fighting it?' Zakahr suggested. 'Why would you resist something so nice?'

'I'm a mother-to-be!' She tried to make a joke, but Zakahr didn't smile.

'So—soon you can be responsible, soon you can stay in every night…' He voiced everything that she wanted to happen, everything she feared. 'You can say goodbye to your passionate—'

'I'm really not,' Lavinia said. If he knew how boring she was he'd run a mile.

'I dispute that.'

'Are you saying I should just walk away from Rachael? That I should give up…?'

'Of course not,' Zakahr said. 'But you are single *now*. You can be selfish. You can do what you want. And,' he said, 'you want *me*.'

It wasn't a question. It was nothing she could deny. Because so very badly she *did*.

'You told me with your mouth.'

'It was just a kiss.'

'With your tongue.'

She just stood there.

'With your hips,' Zakahr said, and watched her redden at the memory of her groin pressing into his. It was as if it were now, her body flaring as she stood, and he refused to leave it there. 'You told me with your hand,' Zakahr said, and in a cruel repeat he did what he had before—but without her guidance this time.

She watched, curious, fascinated, wanting, as he

raised his hand slowly, slipped it inside her jacket. Her nipple jutted through the sheer fabric to greet him. He rested his forehead on her head, and for Lavinia the relief was exquisite.

All night she'd denied this, all day she'd remembered—and now she got to relive it.

'Why *do* you fight it?' Zakahr asked, but even as she tried to fathom an answer, even as she tried to do just that, he overrode her with a single word. 'Don't.'

'Don't?'

'Don't fight it.' Zakahr stroked slowly, and when still she stood he slipped his hand up her cami to the heaven of no padding, no bra, just the taut swell of her.

Lavinia ached for more contact. She could feel the throb between her legs. But she just held his gaze. She would not stop him, because so badly she wanted him, but he would do nothing more till she begged it of him.

When he held her she forgot not to trust him.

Zakahr liked sex.

Not the build-up to it, nor the come-down after it—though no lover of Zakahr's could tell. He was detached, he performed, he got what he needed, she got what she wanted.

But here, in this stand-off, he was loving the build-up, was here, right here in the moment, aroused by her pleasure.

He stroked on till her neck arched backwards. He stroked on till her lips clamped hard on her plea. He stroked on till it was Zakahr who ached for more contact.

He pushed up her cami, saw her pretty naked breast, and lowered his head.

Lavinia could not believe the bliss of it, the thrill of it. There was nowhere to go but backwards. She leant on the fabric behind, his mouth her only contact, and she watched.

She watched his tongue flick her nipple, watched him softly blow, closed her eyes as he suckled, and then watched again as he drew his lips back on the length of her nipple.

He was so hard. There was no choice for Zakahr but to cease contact—and for Lavinia there was both regret and relief when he did.

'I have to go.'

'You don't.'

'Actually, I do.' Lavinia pulled down her top. She could see a damp circle form as the fabric met her breast, and pulled her jacket over to cover it. 'I'm meeting Rachael…' This was madness, she knew—just madness. 'I'm supposed to be proving to Ms Hewitt what a responsible woman I am.' Her voice choked at the irony of it all.

'I could come with you,' Zakahr said. 'Perhaps if she thought you were in a steady relationship…'

'Steady!' She shot out an incredulous laugh. 'You've got *temporary* written all over you.'

He didn't even try to deny it.

It was madness, Lavinia told herself again. Dangerous too. 'I have to go.'

She practically ran—which was just as well, because Zakahr too craved distance.

What the hell was wrong with him? That he'd even suggested going with her was... He was cross with himself as he strode back towards the lift. Cross that now another afternoon would be wasted, pondering the mystery of her, another night of ruing her games. He wanted her in his bed, not his head.

'This just came.'

The receptionist rushed over, and Zakahr took the thick gold envelope, recognising its royal seal. But his mind was still on Lavinia as he scanned the invitation.

She was way too distracting, Zakahr decided.

Then he read the invitation again, and decided maybe some distraction was merited—just not at work.

An idea was forming, and his lips stretched in an unseen smile as a plan took shape. Back in the office, Zakahr picked up the phone—and then glanced at his watch, realising it was too early to make a call to the UK. But with his decision made he fired off an e-mail to Abigail—he had already put her on standby: it would come as little surprise that he wanted her to join him immediately.

Then he made another call, delivered a rapid RSVP to the lavish invitation while flicking through the photos of Rula and admiring the private secretary's discretion as he went through the finer details.

Actually, it would be great having Abigail here, Zakahr decided, as Lavinia's phone rang out again and again, till finally it diverted to his. Abigail didn't take endless breaks, and if she was away she ensured that at least his calls were covered.

'Belenki!'

'Sorry, Zakahr…'

He clicked on his pen as someone in Legal asked if he had signed the contracts. He was about to say yes, to tell them they could send someone to come and get them, then he looked again at the photos on his desk. He thought of an already too-thin Lavinia, who had been considered too big for Kolovsky, and then Zakahr thought again.

'I'm not signing them.'

There was a beat of silence, followed by a shout of incredulous laughter, then a suggestion that he was joking.

Zakahr assured the voice on the phone that he wasn't.

CHAPTER NINE

ALL of it—*all* of it—would be made so much easier if only Lavinia was sure Rachael wanted her.

Lavinia picked her up from her foster family—saw her pinched little mistrusting face peeking out from behind her foster mother's leg.

'She's tired,' Rowena said, after introducing herself, and then told her a little of Rachael's day. 'She's had a big morning at kindergarten.'

'I won't keep her out long.' Lavinia forced a smile she couldn't feel as she offered her hand, but her sister didn't take it.

Rachael trailed Lavinia to her car and quietly let herself be strapped in. 'I thought we could go for a milkshake,' Lavinia said brightly.

'I hate milk.'

'Since when?' Lavinia grinned, but Rachael didn't answer.

'Maybe we could go to a park?'

Which was far easier said than done. Lavinia had no idea of the local area, and they ended up on a rather sad strip of faded grass, with a slide, a rickety old see-saw and two swings—not even a duck in sight.

'Is Rowena nice?' Lavinia attempted, when Rachael climbed down from her dutiful swing, but Rachael just shrugged.

'I *am* trying to get things sorted for you,' Lavinia started, but there were so many things Ms Hewitt had said not to discuss with her.

'How?' Rachael asked.

'I just am.' Lavinia had to settle for that. 'Let's go on the see-saw.'

'Before you take me back?'

They didn't even last the hour. Lavinia tried to console herself it was because Rachael was tired, but the reality was that their time together was hard work.

'I'll try and see you again next week,' Lavinia said, not wanting to make promises Ms Hewitt might not let her keep. Securing her into her seat, she went to give Rachael a kiss, but she pulled her head away.

She dropped her back to the foster home, gave her a hug that wasn't returned, and, driving back to work Lavinia, who never cried, was precariously close to it. She'd had so much pinned on that hour, and there were so many things she had wanted to say. Nothing had transpired. If anything, Rachael was more distant than before.

She dashed to the loo in the foyer, blew her noise, touched up her make-up—though she needn't have bothered.

No one even noticed Lavinia enter the office, so furious was the argument taking place. The room seemed filled with people from Legal, Accounts and, loudest of all, Katina.

'*N'et.*' Katina's lips were white with rage. 'You cannot do this! It's too late. You *cannot* do this.'

'I'm not doing anything,' came Zakahr's clipped response. And, just as Lavinia had surmised on the first day, he didn't shout, didn't raise his voice—such was his authority he simply didn't need to. Zakahr overrode everyone.

'You *have* to sign!' Katina insisted. 'You have to—'

'I don't *have* to do anything,' Zakahr interrupted, and Lavinia froze in realisation. The shots of Rula were scattered over his desk, but Zakahr was ignoring them. As chaos reigned around him he was typing away at his laptop as if there was nothing more annoying than a fly in the room.

'You're trying to ruin the House of Kolovsky,' Katina spat. 'You tried before, with your cheap suggestions to Nina, and now…' Katina was so furious she tripped over her words. 'Now with this decision you will ruin it.'

'Why?' Now Zakahr *did* look up. 'Because I refuse to endorse a few images? *This*—' his manicured hand swept the photos on the table '—is not the vision I have for Kolovsky. Now, if you'll excuse me, I have work to do. I suggest you have the same.'

Katina cried.

One of the hardest women Lavinia knew actually cried as she left the room.

'That's months of work you've just destroyed,' Lavinia said when they were alone; her heart was thumping in her chest yet Zakahr seemed unmoved. He stood and stared out of the window, down to the city streets below.

Maybe, Lavinia reasoned, he just didn't comprehend what he had just done—or maybe, and she paled at the very thought, maybe Katina was right…

'*Are* you here to destroy Kolovsky?'

'You're being ridiculous.'

'Am I?' Lavinia asked. 'You tried to destroy it before.' She watched as his shoulders stiffened. 'When Nina didn't know you were her son you bombarded her with ridiculous suggestions—you were going to put a Kolovsky *bedlinen* range in supermarkets…'

'A one-off!' Zakahr did not turn. 'With a portion of profit going to my charity. Why would I want to destroy what I own?'

'Because you hate her?'

Hate was a word that sounded wrong coming from Lavinia; there was no venom behind it, just a bewildered question.

'What is it with the overreaction?' He turned, irritated now. 'This has nothing to do with my family or destroying Kolovsky. Why the melodrama? I've said that Rula can come back for a re-shoot when she is a healthier weight, or they can find another model. I refuse to put my signature on a page that encourages a seventeen-year-old girl to starve.'

'You can't change the industry.'

'Really?' Zakahr frowned. 'I thought I just did.'

Her questions had been too close for comfort; Zakahr dismissed her with a turn of his head and stared unseeing out of the thick windows, only resting his forehead on the cool glass when he heard the door close behind Lavinia. To keep up the façade it would have made more sense just to sign. A week or so from now it would be over anyway—there would be no Face of Kolovsky—yet he could not put his name to this madness, could not condone what his parents had.

He turned as the door opened and Lavinia entered.

'I've thought about it, and you're right.' Her words surprised him. Her opinion should not matter, and neither did he need her approval, yet even if not sought there was a curious pleasure in having it. 'I was wrong,' Lavinia added. 'You can make a difference.'

'How was lunch?' Zakahr asked, changing the subject, because guilt was a visitor he did not welcome. She trusted him, Zakahr realized. Trusted in his decisions, trusted that his intentions were for the greater good. For the first time he had trouble meeting her eyes.

'Spent bouncing up and down on a see-saw.' Lavinia smiled, but it changed midway. Somehow she just couldn't feign happy right now. 'It was hard work,' Lavinia admitted. 'Maybe I'm kidding myself—maybe she doesn't even want to live with me…'

'Don't doubt yourself.'

'It's hard not to,' Lavinia choked. 'She doesn't want to spend time with me.'

He did not want to get involved with this part of her—he wanted only Lavinia the woman. Yet she came with a whole lot more, and Zakahr knew his insight could help. Surely he could share that without getting involved?

'She resents you,' Zakahr said.

'Me?'

'You come in dressed in your gorgeous clothes,

smelling of perfume, like some fairytale princess come to rescue her, and then you send her back.'

'I have no choice.'

'I'm just telling you how she feels,' Zakahr said. 'She would probably prefer that you do not come.'

God, he could be brutal.

'How can you *say* that?'

Because he knew it. Because he'd lived it. Zakahr gave a rare piece of himself.

'When I was in Detsky Dom a family looked to adopt me. I was a good-looking child, clever...' Zakahr's voice was analytical. 'For two weekends they came and took me out. I stayed in their hotel—they wanted me to enjoy, to be grateful, to laugh...' His eyes were actually darker, if that was possible, almost black with the memory of many years ago.

'So I shouldn't visit?' She hated what he was saying, but she hated the ramifications more—couldn't stand the thought of not visiting Rachael. Again she had read him wrong.

'You *never* miss a visit,' Zakahr said. 'No matter how rude, how appalling her behaviour, how ungrateful she is, *always* you are there. She's testing you,' he said. 'She's waiting for you to prove that she's right.'

'Right about what?'

'That you don't really love her—that one day you will turn your back. Rachael is testing you. To her, she's just expediting the inevitable process.'

'I'm not going to change my mind.'

'Good—because while you were out Ms Hewitt rang,' Zakahr said, and watched her eyes widen. 'She only got as far as speaking with Reception, but she is ringing back next week for a reference check. That must mean they are seriously considering you.'

And suddenly ruined photoshoots and skinny models and tricky access visits, even the stunning man before her, all faded as a long-held dream perhaps began to be realised.

'I could be getting her…' Lavinia was actually shaking. 'They're actually taking my application seriously.' Her hand moved to her mouth as the news sank in. 'I could have her next week.'

'Don't go racing ahead…'

'I could, though.'

'Then you should enjoy this weekend,' Zakahr said. 'You more than impressed the King. He doesn't want to reciprocate with dinner—he has a yacht chartered in Sydney, his family are enjoying their visit, and he has asked us to join him on the yacht on Saturday, stay overnight as his guests.'

That brought Lavinia back to earth—a shaky earth, a changing earth, an earth that moved beneath her feet, that blew her towards Zakahr whenever he reached for her.

'We can't.' Lavinia shook her head.

'It would surely be rude to refuse such an offer?'

'You can easily refuse.' Lavinia's mind flailed at the prospect. She wanted to say yes, but was scared to. 'You don't have to say yes. The King would understand…'

'Maybe I want to say yes.'

She heard her own swallow as Zakahr paused.

'Perhaps you want to too?'

She had to tell him—had to somehow find the words to explain that the woman he saw, the sensual woman he had held, only came to life by his hand.

'It is separate rooms?'

'Of course.' Zakahr sounded affronted. 'The King would not be so crass.'

Finally she could breathe—but only for a second.

'I will ring his aide.'

'I haven't said yes.'

'Then say no.'

She was trapped. Not by his directness, but by her own desire. Trapped because even if he was dangerous, even if she should say no, even if she knew he would soon break her heart, for the first time in her life Lavinia wanted to say yes—wanted to give in to the call of desire.

'Don't assume...' Lavinia attempted.

'I never assume,' Zakahr said.

Which he didn't.

He just *knew*.

CHAPTER TEN

'How's your daughter?' Lavinia asked Eddie as he held the limousine door open for her. Today she was the guest of a king, today she was the 'plus one' of Zakahr, so there was no question of her driving. But his limousine was out of place at eight a.m. on Saturday in her ordinary suburban street.

'I'm a grandfather!' Eddie gave a proud smile, but it was a touch wan. 'They've called her Emily—she's tiny, but a real fighter.'

She would have to be. Lavinia knew that Emily had been born not only premature, but with a heart condition that would need surgery. 'This is for Emily.' Lavinia said, and handed him a package and then another smaller one. 'And this is for Princess Jasmine, so it's to go on the plane. Can you tell them to be careful with it, as it's fragile?'

As is your heart, her inner voice warned as she climbed into the limousine. To her surprise, she saw that Zakahr was there.

'I thought we'd be coming to pick you up.'

'You are my guest today and tonight,' Zakahr said. 'And shall be treated as such.'

Even so, she took the seat opposite him. The implication, however subtle, was there—she was not his PA today but his guest, and she would be his lover...a woefully inexperienced lover. Somehow she had to find the courage to tell him.

Wanted to tell him.

Wanted him.

Lavinia turned her head away, tried to think of something light and witty to say, but nothing was forthcoming. She knew she was playing with fire, knew all about the heartbreak reputation she was ill-equipped to handle, but for the first time in her life there was a man who didn't evoke her usual caution—there were feelings, experiences that she wanted to explore, and she could only envisage doing it with him.

She could handle it, Lavinia had told herself when she'd accepted his offer, and, really, since then she'd been too busy to think.

Everything would be taken care of, Zakahr had assured her. She did not have to do anything other than choose her wardrobe. And, given she had the Kolovsky design team at her disposal, and because he was male, he assumed it was as easy as that. Yet, as a female, the moment she had said yes to his dizzying offer a frantic dash to the imaginary finishing line had ensued.

Yes, her wardrobe had been skilfully sorted by Katina, but there had been stockings, panties and new lipstick to buy, a trip to the hairdresser's, then a last minute bikini wax to ensure that *all* her hair was neatly taken care of. And then the extremely difficult task of buying a small gift for someone who literally had everything!

All Zakahr had had to do was roll out of bed.

He hadn't even shaved.

She flicked her eyes to him, and then back out of the window. Her heart was leaping, as was her stomach, at the daunting sight of him. She had only ever seen him in a suit, but Zakahr in smart-casual was just as giddying—perhaps more so. He was, from her quick peek, wearing charcoal-grey linen trousers and a white fitted shirt—impossibly elegant, dangerously relaxed, achieving effortlessly what Lavinia had spent the past hours striving for.

'Will it be very grand?' Lavinia asked, nervous not only at the prospect of Zakahr.

'The King is supposed to be a marvellous host, so I'm sure it will be pleasurable. You got on well with Jasmine at dinner.'

The journey was awkward—so much so that in the end Lavinia opened the partition and spoke with Eddie, asking more about his granddaughter and sympathising with him as to the stressful times that lay ahead.

Zakahr checked his e-mails, trying not to listen, trying not to hear that Eddie's son-in-law was taking time off work to be there for his wife and new daughter, and that Eddie was stepping in to help them out financially, so they could concentrate on Emily rather than worry about bills.

He did not want to hear it.

Would not *let* himself hear it.

He did this month in, month out—year in, year out. It was no different from any of the other companies he had closed—still, it was a relief when they turned off for the airport, bypassing all car parks and queues.

For once it was Lavinia being driven straight on to the tarmac, but only as she climbed the steps to a small jet did a different set of nerves catch up—an unexpected set of nerves. For a second she stalled.

'Okay?' Zakahr checked as he walked up the stairs behind her, and Lavinia forced legs that felt like jelly to move forward, smiling to the waiting cabin crew and stepping inside.

It was divine, but it did not soothe—not the plush leather seats or the thick carpet. As she sat, even idle conversation wasn't happening, and she wished he'd flick open a newspaper so she could just close her eyes and go into herself as the plane started taxiing. But instead Zakahr was looking at her as Lavinia tightened the strap over her lap.

'Are you a nervous flyer?'

'It would appear so.'

'It's only an hour.'

It was going to be the longest hour of her life, and Lavinia blew out a long breath at the prospect.

'Why didn't you say something before?' Zakahr frowned. 'You could have taken something—'

'I didn't know,' Lavinia interrupted, and then turned to him. 'I've never flown.'

'Never?'

'I've never been to Sydney either.' Lavinia was more than a little embarrassed by her admission, and to mask that her voice came out a little more snappish that she had intended. 'So don't expect me to play tour guide.'

Again she had surprised him. He'd been sure that she was used to being whisked away. But she was like a glorious butterfly, cooped up in Kolovsky and unable to fly.

'It's very safe.'

'Sure.'

Zakahr recalled *his* first flight; there had been no nerves, just the feeling of excitement that he was finally on his way to make real his dreams. An elderly man sitting next to him had talked to him, so Zakahr did the same now. He told Lavinia about that first flight, when he had been a teenager, on his way to England, hardly speaking the language, hoping that an old friend from the orphanage he had contacted would be meeting him, his nerves that Immigration would turn him around.

He did something else too.

Zakahr held her hand as he spoke, and she could feel it hot and dry around her cold one, and instead of worrying about the noise and the speed she was listening, trying to imagine being so young and so brave.

A light breakfast was served, and still he spoke. Lavinia chose warmed blueberries smothered in cold yoghurt, the ripe fruit bursting on her tongue, and she finally got her champagne, with a small hibiscus flower placed inside the glass that slowly unfurled as the bubbles streamed over it. And it wasn't just the flower opening up under her genuine interest. So too did Zakahr.

'How did you start?' Lavinia asked. 'If you had no formal qualifications?'

'I lied.' A slow smile spread over his face. 'Only at first. I didn't have to for long. I was clever, I had confidence—people respond to that.' He told her how he had waited on tables and cleaned houses for a year, studying not just the language but his options, working out what it would take to get on that first step of a golden ladder, then buying a second-hand suit. 'Not any suit,' Zakahr said. 'I found good second-hand shops. That suit was more expensive than a regular new suit, but with the right shoes, the right briefcase, the right haircut, the right address…'

'The right address?'

'I made sure I cleaned at the right address. Every morning at ten the letters landed on the mat.'

Lavinia gaped at how he had reinvented himself.

'For one year I saved for my interview outfit. I had three shirts, five ties, one suit… With my first pay packet I bought another second-hand suit; after one year I had my first suit tailor made. I had no need to lie about my qualifications then. I knew that once I was in they would not want to lose me.'

'Wow!' Lavinia blinked. 'I can see I've gone the boring way about it.'

'Boring?' Zakahr questioned, because here was a woman who never had bored him.

'I'm not brave enough to lie,' Lavinia said. 'Anyway, I actually needed that bit of paper to get in to university.' She saw she wasn't making much sense. 'When I finished school I went to TAFE part-time.'

'TAFE?'

'Like college,' Lavinia said. 'I finished my schooling, but it took for ever—four years, part-time.'

'You still study?'

'Chemistry.' Lavinia nodded. 'Though that's happening ever slower—more so if I get Rachael. At this rate, by the time I'm thirty I'll have my degree and be teaching.'

'You're studying for a Chemistry degree?'

'Painfully slowly,' Lavinia admitted. 'But, yes.'

It was like watching a pleasing movie and then being handed 3D glasses. All the colours, all the nuances that were Lavinia, were amplified with every look, and he knew that there was more. Normally it would have troubled him—for when it wasn't business Zakahr never wanted more detail, never wanted extra involvement. Only with Lavinia he did.

They were preparing for descent, the short journey over, their table cleared. Aware she would be nervous, he carried on talking and offered his hand. But she just laughed and didn't accept.

'I'm not nervous any more.' Lavinia grinned. 'The closer we get, the better I feel. I think I rather like flying after all.'

She just adapted, Zakahr realised, staring out of the window. Sydney was spread out in the most stunning riot of ocean and rocks, and it was impossible to see this view and not be moved. He could smell her hair as she leant over him, could feel her elbow in his chest as she drank in the view. And he didn't want her to pull back, would have loved to undo the belts and pull her onto his lap.

As Lavinia moved back to her seat, her cheek moved past Zakahr's face, and whether it was his will or want she hesitated, turned to him with eyes that were crystal-clear. Contact would be both the solution and the problem—releasing a volatile energy she wasn't sure she could deal with. But how she wanted to…

It was Lavinia who kissed him, but there was nothing bold about it—no first move—because the moves had long since been made.

She kissed lips that she wanted, that wanted her, she tasted champagne on his tongue and the only place in her mind was *here*.

There was an awakening within her that he had triggered—one she had suppressed, one she had ignored, one that needed to come to its own natural conclusion. Like caesium reacting with water, her body fizzed and danced on the surface of his caress. He spoke her name into her mouth and his fingers bunched in her hair, and he kissed her deeper, with the delicious warning of intent, his mouth more possessive now, telling her without words that tonight would be explosive.

But first there was a truth that needed to be told. She had to untangle her lips from his, every cell protesting at the disengagement, but she knew that her provocation, the bold, sensual woman he'd kissed, was a product only of *him*, and tonight it would be too late to reveal.

'This could be a weekend of firsts…' Lavinia pulled her mouth away a smudge, and Zakahr smiled in triumph at her confirmation that tonight they would finally be lovers.

'Zakahr…' She didn't know how to just come out and say it—so, being Lavinia, she just came out and said it. 'It will be my first time.'

'You haven't been on a yacht?'

'No,' Lavinia said, and it was an impatient no. 'Well, yes—I *haven't* been on a yacht…' It would be far easier to go on kissing him than to say it. 'That's not what I meant.' She took a breath. 'I haven't slept with anyone.'

'Lavinia…' He actually smiled at the impossibility. 'I think we both know—'

'*What* do you know, Zakahr?' Lavinia asked. 'Or what do you assume?'

It was only then that he realised she was being serious—except it made absolutely no sense.

'I know all the rumours. I know people assume I was sleeping with Aleksi, some think Levander too, but they're just that—rumours. People judge me because I can have a laugh, a flirt. Because of my past people just assume that I'm easy, cheap…' She shot him a look. 'You did.'

'I did not,' Zakahr immediately corrected her, because even if his relationships were generally without substance there was no disrespect for the women who had been his lovers. Sex was a necessary reward, and Zakahr would have loved to give more of himself to each and every one of them, but there was no self to give. 'I assumed from *your* actions,' Zakahr went on, 'that you wanted me as I wanted you. It was not your refusal that offended, but the mixed messages, Lavinia.' He could not get his head around it. 'You cannot go around leading—'

'I don't,' Lavinia said. 'I've only ever been like that with you.'

Her words hung between them as they came in to

land. Lavinia leant back in her seat at the force of landing, though it was pale in comparison to the power of the man beside her.

There was no second offer of his hand, his distance immediate. He had thought her teasing at first, but now he knew he was hearing the truth, and it was too much for Zakahr.

'I am not looking for a relationship.' As the plane slowed down, he turned to her. His sentence was curt, but there was nothing lost in translation—he wanted the coming weeks over, and he wanted no part of the family that still invited him in. He did not want his mother, or his siblings—he wanted distraction, not involvement. Lavinia was to have been a stunning reprieve in grim proceedings.

Zakahr wanted Lavinia, but he wanted the silver-eyeshadowed, smart-talking Lavinia—the one who laughed and poked her tongue out at the world, who knew men, knew the rules that he could deal with. What he struggled with was the *other* Lavinia—the Lavinia who seemed to be dragging him into a world that he had always refused to inhabit. Lavinia oozed feeling and emotion. Zakahr did his best to avoid both. Yet there was no one without the other with the woman beside him.

'Was I asking for a relationship?'

'Please…' He halted, because again he was assuming—but it was an assumption based on long history. Always women wanted more than he could even begin to give.

'Can't we just see what happens? Any day now I could have Rachael.'

Zakahr closed his eyes, and Lavinia had the temerity to laugh as his face paled.

'Zakahr—it's because of that that I don't want a relationship with *you*. I might take a risk with my own heart, but never with hers,' she said. 'I know the sort of family I want to give Rachael—' it was Lavinia's turn to be brutal '—and that's something you could never provide.'

There was a conversation there, but he chose not to pursue it—he did not want to hear what he could not give. The crew were out now, the cabin door was opening, and he could see the car and the King's aide waiting on the tarmac. Zakahr unclipped his belt, just wanting the hell out, but Lavinia caught his arm.

'I want to be twenty-four…' She caught his eyes and stared into them, and to the dangerous place beyond. 'I am in no position to have a relationship, but I want to be with you. I want one night…' She didn't know the words, she didn't know how to articulate—to tell him that even if she must accept he wasn't interested in for ever still she wanted *now*. 'For one day, one night, I want to forget so that I can remember.'

He could not respond. He did not know how to respond—because he wanted more than one night. He had been going to propose a full week—a week that would both resolve his past and secure her future.

'Zakahr…'

He pulled his hand away and then stood. Only then did he respond. 'As I said on our first day—you have no idea who you're playing with.' He shook his head in disbelief, angry with her for her misplaced trust. 'Again, I tell you—you need to be more careful.'

There was no chance for further discussion.

The King's aide met them on the tarmac, and they were driven to the wharf, making polite conversation along the way but never to each other.

Lavinia could feel his tension, knew he felt beguiled, and only as they stepped out of the car and walked along the jetty towards the yacht was there a chance for terse conversation.

'You should have told me.'

'It's not something you just slip into the conversation. When was I supposed to tell you?'

'In the car park it might have—'

'I'd known you less than a week!' Lavinia retorted, but her cheeks were burning as she recalled their blistering kiss—hardly her usual response to a virtual stranger. 'Oh, well.' Lavinia tossed her hair. 'Just because I'm off-limits on your strange moral compass, it doesn't mean we can't enjoy our time here.'

It would, Zakahr quickly realised, be *impossible* to enjoy his time here.

As they boarded they were warmly greeted by the King and his family. Jasmine, amongst her own family and in the privacy of the yacht, was unveiled, revealing a smiling, happy face, and she was clearly delighted to see Lavinia again—a completely different woman from the shy Princess they had first met. Their laughter filled the salty air, reaching Zakahr's ears as he took refreshment with the King on deck.

The stunning vehicle that was to be their home till tomorrow was soon moving out of Darling Harbour, and though it was a visual feast—the huge Harbour Bridge, the splendour of the Opera House—it wasn't the scenery that over and over again forced his gaze. It was Lavinia—completely at ease with the royals, delighted in her surroundings, and the company he wanted to be keeping. He had, as Lavinia had pointed out, *assumed*.

Not just from her job, or the rumours, but from her bold kisses, from the desire of her body—yet her purity muddied the waters for Zakahr.

He liked *uncomplicated*—would soon be walking away. A brief, albeit passionate, affair with Lavinia would have eased the stress of the day. This, though, however she denied it, was teetering Lavinia-style towards a relationship.

Refreshments taken, they were shown by staff to their accommodation. Yes, Zakahr realised, this day and night would be more than impossible—it would be hell. And, thanks to his careful instructions when he'd accepted the invitation, it was a hell of his own making.

Lavinia had no idea what to expect—for not only hadn't she flown, apart from a trip on the ferry to Tasmania she had never been on a boat, and the yacht they had boarded outreached even her wildest imaginings. It was as luxurious as any five-star hotel. They had walked through a lounge filled with scattered sofas, and a huge bar with large plasma screens, and there was a vast dining area where, Jasmine told her, they would dine tonight. But lunch would be served on deck. There was even a dance floor.

As they took the steps down to the next level an aide took Zakahr to his suite and a female aide took Lavinia further along a narrow corridor. And though it was becoming clearer by the moment how luxurious this trip would be, Lavinia gaped in awe when she first glimpsed her suite.

A large four-poster bed was the centrepiece, with heavy walnut furniture, thick carpets and a dressing table. There was even a sunken spa.

'It's stunning!' She roamed the vast suite, opening doors, admiring her already unpacked clothes and her toiletries set out in the bathroom. 'What's this…?' she asked, stopping in front of another door.

'Adjoining,' Mara the aide said, lowering her eyes. 'The King understands there are differences…' Clearly a little embarrassed, Mara explained that lunch would served shortly on deck and left.

It was very like having a red button with a sign saying not to push it—only it wasn't Lavinia resisting temptation, it was Zakahr. Refusing to be embarrassed, Lavinia gave the wooden door a sharp rap, and then opened it to find Zakahr lying scowling on his bed, gorgeous in the dark grey linen pants and white shirt, sulky and thoroughly fed up with his lot.

'Hi there, neighbour!'

He didn't reply.

'Don't worry—I shan't be creeping in at night. You can sleep safely.'

'Ha-ha,' came Zakahr's response.

'Sorry to rot up your plans.' Lavinia perched on the end of his bed. 'But I told you not to assume…'

Zakahr shuttered his eyes. She was right—he *had* assumed. So much so that now he had Abigail arriving on Monday. His intention had been to have Lavinia safely tucked up in his bed for the remainder of his stay in Australia, distraction merited, but only at night. He looked over to where she sat. How much easier would it be to just reach out and pull her towards him? There was almost a thread between them in that moment—one that could draw them closer or snap—and Zakahr knew he had to break it. For there could be no involvement. They were from two different worlds, opposite sides of the world, and soon Lavinia would be carer to a child. Zakahr had tried relationships. They did not suit at the best of times, and this, for Zakahr, was the worst of times.

'If you've waited this long you should wait to be with someone you're serious…' He couldn't finish, because he couldn't stand the thought of a future Mr Lavinia—or, worse, a one-night stand because she didn't want to be alone, with some lowlife who wouldn't take care of her.

'We'd better go up for lunch.' Lavinia stood. 'Imagine them giving us adjoining rooms—I can't imagine why they thought us a couple.' She gave him a wink before closing the door. 'See you on deck.'

It was a casual lunch, with Lavinia chatting with Jasmine and her bridesmaids as waiters mingled with plates—and it was lovely to be out on the water, to be away from her problems for a little while.

'He's very handsome!' Lavinia looked at a photo of Jasmine's husband-to-be.

'I know.' Jasmine smiled. 'Lucky for me I am the youngest of five girls. My father had a lot more say in my older sisters' husbands—and he was not my father's first choice for me. He is a friend of my brother's,' Jasmine explained. 'They were at university together, and sometimes he would come to the palace. I had a terrible crush on him for years. My brother spoke with my father a few months ago, told him how unhappy I would be if I followed *his* choice. I am very blessed to have such a wonderful family.'

The Princess smiled as Zakahr walked over and joined them, and though she returned it, for a second Lavinia struggled: it was things like that that hurt at times. Lavinia certainly didn't show it—but so many times she'd wondered how much easier things might have been if there had been brothers and sisters by her side. Even now her world seemed so small—there were friends, of course, but those friends had their own families. She ached sometimes, literally ached, for a sister to ring her up, or have coffee with her, a family to moan about too, to visit for Christmas and birthdays.

'I was just saying to Lavinia how nice it is to come from a large family.' Jasmine politely invited him into the conversation.

Zakahr respectfully declined.

'It is my pleasure to meet them.'

They spoke for a few minutes about the King's cousin, who spent four months a year in Australia. It was his boat they were on. They spoke, but they only talked, and

Lavinia realised then that had she not known his past he would never have revealed it—saw first-hand just how little Zakahr let anyone in.

'I need to speak with my father.'

Jasmine excused herself, and Zakahr revealed the real reason he had come over—he had seen Lavinia's slender shoulders pinken, seen her nose and cheeks redden a touch, and even if she wasn't to be his lover she promoted reluctant responsibility. 'You need to apply sunblock.'

'I know!' Lavinia whispered. 'I forgot to bring any.'

'Ask Jasmine if she has some…' His voice trailed off. Jasmine's skin was lovely and brown; it was Lavinia who was lily-white. 'You need it.'

'I'm scared to ask,' Lavinia admitted. 'They're so polite they'll probably go and helicopter some in, or something…'

'I'll sort it.' He was back a few moments later, having had a word with one of the crew, and handed her a tube. 'They will also put some aftersun in your cabin.'

'Hardly a cabin!' Lavinia smiled.

People were starting to drift off. The afternoon sun was too fierce to stay on deck, and the King announced that he might sleep for a while. Jasmine wanted to watch a film. Lavinia was on the King's side.

'We meet at seven for dinner,' Jasmine's mother informed them. 'Relax for now, Lavinia. Enjoy the boat, your room…'

They were just the nicest people. Lavinia had been rather worried that she'd have to talk and entertain right up till bedtime, but they were the most lovely hosts. The Queen sat in the shade with a book, Jasmine and her bridesmaids curled up to watch a film, and a very guilt-free Lavinia slipped down the stairs to the cool bliss of her suite. Peeling off her clothes, down to her bra and panties, she winced at her pink shoulders. They didn't hurt yet, but possibly would by evening.

She rubbed in cool aloe vera aftersun lotion, swore never to leave her room again without sunblock, and then stretched out on the bed, enjoying the gentle lulling motion of the yacht. She was relaxed, yet not. Aware that Zakahr was close, deciding that perhaps his reaction to her news was possibly for the best.

She wanted to be made love to by him, she wanted him to be her first, but her assurances to him that she expected nothing were perhaps more what he'd needed to hear than what she had wanted to say.

He captured her mind in a way no man ever had, Lavinia thought as she headed into a lovely long sleep. With him Lavinia was—possibly for the first time in her life—completely herself.

She'd told him of her past, told him of her present, even her hopes for the future.

It wasn't Zakahr who enthralled her.

Neither Belenki the businessman.

Nor the focussed Riminic, who had chosen to reinvent himself, who had Lavinia slightly spellbound.

It was the whole montage of him—the smile that could make her stomach fold, the dark humour and those glimpses of a softer side, a protective side. To have that, to be wrapped in it, to be held by it even for a little while, would be hell to let go of.

'Lavinia?'

He *so* did not want to go in there, but it was after six, and there were no noises from her room, so Zakahr realised that it was up to him to wake her. Unlike Lavinia, Zakahr did not relish down-time—he had no desire to make small-talk with his hosts, nor did he know how to relax. Bed in the afternoon was what he had hoped for— but not alone. He had taken off his shirt and stretched out on the bed, and spent a restless afternoon playing heads or tails with his conscience, thinking what they should be doing now. On too many occasions had come dangerously close to her door.

What was preventing him, Zakahr was not quite sure.

He had broken many hearts in his past, and Lavinia was willing—there was a strange sense of honour that kept him back, though. A sense of the damage he could wreak, a wanting to spare her from the hurt that was inevitably to come.

'Lavinia!' He knocked again and then pushed it open. 'It's after six.'

She jolted awake with the horrible realisation that she had less than an hour to get ready to dine with the King, and with no Katina on hand or a hairdresser to help this time. Sun, sea and a champagne breakfast had ensured Lavinia slept well—now she heard the sound of laughter from above, and a rap at the adjoining door, saw Zakahr standing in the doorway.

'Oh, God…' Lavinia did her best not to dwell on the splendid sight of him—naked from the waist up, he was more beautiful than her many imaginings. His pale skin was shadowed with a smatter of chest hair like a charcoal smudge that led down to the now crumpled linen trousers; he looked sulky, restless and never more beautiful. But it was easier to snap than to admit it… 'Why didn't you wake me?' Her high, terse voice was a contrast to his drawl.

'I'm trying to give up the habit!'

There was no time to think of a reply. Lavinia jumped off the bed, wincing as her bra strap stuck into her sunburnt shoulders, then wincing for a different reason as Zakahr turned to go and she caught sight of the scars that laced his back, the ripple of muscles rising beneath almost in defiance.

He must have heard her intake of breath, or just realised he'd left himself exposed, because she watched those muscles stiffen, saw his neck turn a fraction, as if to witness her response, but then he changed his mind, closing the door behind him, and Lavinia stood for a moment, trying to take in not just what she had just seen but her own response to it.

Lavinia never cried.

At five years of age she had worked out that tears were entirely wasted—that it was far more productive to just smile and carry on.

She *chose* happiness—forcibly wrenched herself from bitterness and anger, yet it drenched her now. There was fury that shot towards Nina, that ricocheted to Ivan, to all of them, to anyone who had touched him—a possessive fury she had met before when she'd heard about the bruises on Rachael.

Except this was a man, Lavinia told herself. A man who did not need her protection and certainly did not want her compassion or her heart.

So she did what she did best—swallowed unshed tears, applied make-up to her sunburn, and then concentrated on her hair and face. She had just slipped on her dress, a trifle worried she would be overdressed, when Zakahr knocked at her door.

'We should go up.'

She hadn't overdressed, Lavinia realised, because Zakahr would never get such things wrong. For dinner he had shaved, and was now suited, utterly ready to dine with the King—and, she thought as her heart quickened, utterly and completely able to bed her at will. She wanted to fall on him, she wanted to kiss him, she wanted to be pushed on to the bed and be made love to by him. There was nothing virginal about her thoughts.

'Two minutes,' she bargained.

'One,' Zakahr allowed—though she did not need it. His eyes tried not to roam her body as he sat on the couch. She was dressed in black, sheer lace and velvet like thick black grapes, hugging her body, and Zakahr wanted to peel and taste each one. Her blonde hair spilled over her shoulders and she must have just sprayed scent, for there was a potent dose of Lavinia in the air.

'You look nice.' Even Zakahr knew that was too

paltry. 'You look fantastic. The dress…' *The woman in it*, was unspoken, but Zakahr ignored his impulse and kept his voice even. 'The pattern…'

Lavinia laughed. 'Devoré.' She smiled at his nonplussed reaction. 'You've got a lot to learn.'

So did she, Zakahr thought, stamped with a fierce need to teach her, but changing the subject instead. 'What's that?' he asked when, having slipped on high heels, she picked up a wrapped present from her dressing table.

'A gift for Jasmine.'

'I'll arrange a gift on Monday.'

'I'm sure you will!' Lavinia said as she fiddled with her dress in the full-length mirror. 'Or rather you'll ask me to have something very tasteful, beautiful and expensive arranged, to thank the King for his hospitality. This, though—' she turned and smiled '—is just a little present for Jasmine from me!'

Was there an affront there? Zakahr could see no reason for one, yet there was just a slight mockery to her voice that he chose to ignore.

'Let's go.' He stood just as the yacht lurched slightly while it anchored.

Lavinia, grimly holding on to her present with one hand, made a quick grab for the four-poster bed with the other and balanced herself in her heels. And then as easily as that she caught his eye—she did nothing, no dance, nothing provocative, just smiled as she held onto the bedpost.

'I told you—I just can't help myself sometimes.'

And as easily as that he smiled, paused for a second.

There was a short laugh, and then he walked behind her up to the deck—ruing how easily she lightened him, the verbal shorthand that had developed between them, and the irony that for the first time as he walked into a room with a woman, still smiling at their little joke, even if she was out of bounds, it was the closest he had felt to being part of a couple.

The table was elaborate. The Opera House was lit up, a stunning backdrop, and the food and company were exquisite. Surely there should be pride tonight in his achievements—a moment to savour the triumph so close? But the laughter and the company and the woman beside Zakahr found him reluctantly glimpsing an alternative.

There was that unwelcome visitor guilt too, as the meal came to its conclusion. Jasmine and Lavinia were talking between themselves, and Jasmine was opening her present.

'Remember I was telling you about our traditions?'

Lavinia's make-up was fading, and he saw her blush spread down her neck and sun-kissed arms, clearly embarrassed by Jasmine's enthusiasm as she opened the package.

'It's just a tiny little thing. I know you have new, but there are old traditions…'

'It's beautiful.' Jasmine held up the small blue glass horseshoe. It was flimsy and fragile, but had been chosen with so much care. Jasmine was delighted with her gift.

'It is nice to see my daughter make a friend.' As the evening concluded the King strolled on deck with

Zakahr. 'In our position friends are easy to come by—genuine friends are much rarer. I am sure it must be the same for you.'

'It can be,' Zakahr admitted.

They walked for a while, admired the stunning view, but even as they spoke, even as the King bade him goodnight, Zakahr's mind was on Lavinia.

He stared unseeing across the water, realising that the King was right—though for a long time it had suited Zakahr. His position, his wealth, guaranteed he was never short of company—it had suited him, but it just didn't feel so right now. He had suppressed a smile as Lavinia had educated the Princess as to the wonders of social networking, making her promise to post some wedding pictures online, and whether or not Jasmine was being polite, tonight she had agreed. The King was right. They were already friends, and would no doubt stay in touch after the wedding—and then he remembered what tonight he had chosen to forget.

There would be *no* friendship. This time next week the Kolovsky name would be mud to King Abdullah. There would be chaos, and she would be in the thick of it—he had to get her away from there.

CHAPTER ELEVEN

LAVINIA smiled a mirthless smile as, after the most wonderful night, she entered her suite and saw the lit candles.

Petals were scattered on the bed, and even if there had been no alcohol on deck, down below there was champagne, cooling in a bucket. The spa was filled too—all no doubt on Zakahr's instruction, before he'd found out she was a virgin.

She had taken the chance to slip away as Zakahr walked with the King, had said goodnight to her hosts, and now she stood alone and her smile was no longer mirthless. In fact, Lavinia laughed.

She didn't just laugh, she peeled off her dress and shoes and absolutely refused misery, popping the champagne cork and then stripping off her bra and panties.

Zakahr heard her as he walked past and so badly he wanted to join her—to make love to her and, yes, whether she understood it now or at some time in the future, to take care of her in the only way he knew how.

He went into his suite, took off his tie. There was a large brandy waiting for him, which he downed in one, but it did not make a dent. No drink could douse his emotions tonight—but it was a different emotion that rose now, as he knocked on the adjoining door and waited.

Lavinia lay in the spa, champagne in hand, heart in her throat, more than ready to say yes, which she did in a voice that was just a little breathless.

'You've been busy,' Lavinia said as he walked in and slowly took off his jacket. 'I thought you were walking with the King, not stripping roses of their petals and rushing around lighting candles.'

He looked at the candles, the petals, the bubbling spa, and then to her.

'I did a good job!' Zakahr continued the joke. 'I didn't know I could be so romantic.' And then he was serious. 'Are you sure?'

She was absolutely sure.

The bubbles were dispersing, slowly revealing her body to him, and rather than shy she had never felt more sure in her life—Zakahr was the only man she could imagine being like this with. Yes, she had stripped in the past, but she had bared only her body then. With Zakahr she could reveal herself.

'I am a bit scared, though.' She looked up at him and clarified her words. 'Not of you, of *it*.'

'You won't be soon.' It was an assured promise, and even if it still scared her she believed him.

He soaped her arms, her shoulders, her neck, till all traces of make-up were gone, and he saw just how young and vulnerable she was, even if she was tough at times too. He knew she was scared, and was grateful that it was him—because he knew that he would take care of her, knew she would be scared only till he was inside.

He pulled the plug and helped her stand. Lavinia had never been shy of her body, had revealed it too easily, but now, feeling his eyes roam her with affection rather than lust, there was a chasteness that had been missing before, tempting her to cover her breasts as she climbed out of the spa. Instead he pulled her into him, shielded her with his kiss, and feeling his mouth, feeling her hot damp body press into his shirt, for a little while she forgot to be shy.

It was a different kiss than any they'd shared before. Zakahr held her oiled and naked and warm against him, felt her dampen his shirt, and it was another kiss he relished. His hands roamed her waist, her hips, her bottom, her wet hair against his face, till the sheen on her skin evaporated and not even his hands could warm her. He felt her shiver in a mix of exposure and want.

'Come to bed.'

She had never expected tenderness. He pulled back the bedclothes and took off her towel, and she climbed in and lay there, nervous, though not, watching him undress. He slipped off his damp shirt, and there was only beauty tonight in the male form.

Scars and all, he was exquisite. Her eyes feasted on him, and he stood in the warmth of her gaze for a moment before climbing in beside her. For a long while he just held her. Then he turned on his pillow and his mouth found hers.

It was a different kiss again—a slow, tentative kiss to accustom her. And slowly she did—to the feel of being in bed with a man, to a naked body beside her. It was a building kiss, a kiss that spread through her body till it knew what to do. He tasted of brandy—or was it her? A luxurious mingling? Still he kissed her, and her leg slipped against his, felt the roughness of his hair and the solid strength of his thigh, and then his hand slid back to where she had once guided him. He lowered his head, his tongue sliding down her neck. She could feel the wrap of his legs around hers, the scratch of hair between the tender skin of her thighs, and the solid, warm weight of his erection, pressing into her stomach and slipping further down as his body moved. His mouth met her aching nipple and his hand moved lower. He could feel her warmth, feel her trepidation. His mouth worked her breast, and his fingers tenderly probed, and it was Zakahr who was nervous on her behalf. Always he was sheathed, but he thought of her virgin flesh and wanted to *feel* his way in—he wanted all of the experience, and not just for him, so wary was he of hurting her.

'When are you due?' His mouth moved to her ear.

'I'm not… I'm on the pill…'

'Never trust a man when he says this.' Those grey eyes met hers. 'Except me. I have never done anything before without protection.' He never had—had sworn he never would—except he was parting her from her innocence, and he knew that tonight he needed to be more gentle, to feel his way. And he would.

She could trust him.

Not in anything else, but in this she could. And he knew she did.

He had a streetwise side to him, a knowing, a danger

that for tonight was being put on hold. Yes, she could not justify it—she knew some of his depraved past—but it was trust that had led her to his bed, and trust that guided her now.

And it was the same for Zakahr.

So many women had wanted him—all of him. Had thought that a baby would change him—would mellow him. Nothing would.

His tip was moist, and with it Zakahr moistened her. He stroked himself around her and Lavinia lay, her breath high and shallow in her chest, nervous, curious. Then he lowered himself onto her, because he *did* want to kiss her throughout. He kissed her till she was drunk from it, and without ordered thought she was kissing him back. He kissed her till he was in just a little way, and then he kissed her some more.

He held back, but his mind surged forward to pastures new. He wanted her pleasure, he wanted her escape, and without the usual barrier the pleasure was more intense for Zakahr. That he was her first took on vital importance. He whispered words in her ear that were far more than the sweet talk he usually delivered—he whispered words that were dangerous from a man like Zakahr, words he never used.

He told her neck she was beautiful as he licked it, told her cheek he would not hurt her as he kissed it, and inched in just a little deeper, whispering into the shell of her ear that he would *never* hurt her, that she was safe, that she was okay, that he would make it so.

He dizzied her brain with endearments.

He slowly moved and gently she stretched. With each

word, each gentle probe, she opened willingly, and when he completely filled her he showered her senses further with every word she craved. He sounded as if he meant it, so he said it some more, and he felt as if he meant it as her hips rose to greet him, and her lips gasped for air, and her head thrashed with unfamiliar sensation.

Zakahr consumed her, he filled her and he thrust now within her, and it was so breathtakingly wonderful that Lavinia actually wanted it to stop, because she hadn't agreed to this, would never have agreed to this—to the absolute devotion her body held for him, to the complete disregard for the rules she should be abiding by. There could be no holding on to her heart when she was holding on to him.

Her nails dug in his back and her ears accepted his words and her body throbbed beneath his. And then she was coming, and sucking on his skin as he spilled deep within her, and then biting on his shoulder just to stop herself from saying it—because she couldn't, she mustn't. Except she already did… And he was still holding her, and kissing her, and then she rolled and turned away, waiting for it to fade, for sense to prevail. And still she wanted to say it.

Zakahr pulled her warmth towards him, kissed her shoulder and lay there. She was aware for ages that he didn't sleep, that he lay awake beside her, and so many times she had to stop herself from blurting out to the darkness, telling herself it was impossible…

Except it was possible.

She just did.

Already she loved him.

CHAPTER TWELVE

HE WOKE to the absence of regret.

Zakahr noticed because it was usually a familiar bedmate—uneasy with intimacy, he saw it as weakness and always awoke wishing she were gone. Not this morning. Faced away from her, his back exposed, he would normally roll on to his back or climb out of bed. But he had left it too late, because she had already stirred beside him. In silence he lay there, felt her cool hands on his back, felt her fingers tenderly probe his scars, and he braced himself for the inevitable—the demand for information on the strength of one night, as if he were just going to roll over and share the darkest part of his life.

He waited for her questions, but they never came.

Still her hand softly roamed him, and as her fingers explored he relived the hell of each scar, reminded himself why he was right to be here, that the plan in action was deserved. It did not have to affect Lavinia, but that meant he had to trust her, and he tensed at the very thought of it—trust was an enigma to Zakahr.

She felt him tense, but kissed his back, his shoulder, his neck. Lavinia willed him with her mouth to turn to her. Bold, she unfurled beside him, stretching into the new skin of a body that felt different this morning—aware and tender. His skin was warm next to hers, and her hands explored him, past the jut of his hips to the flat of his stomach, inching downwards till she held his morning erection in her hand and adored it. She had been scared—not just last night, maybe all her life—but with him she wasn't any longer. All was beautiful.

Here, now, was where he would turn—here, where he would normally end the intimacy. Yet he lay there and let her explore him, closed his mind to everything but her and then turned to face her. He never wanted to get out of the bed. He felt her mouth kiss his chest and then work down, felt her lips soft, warm and tentative, and then the cool of her tongue. He wanted to give in to her, but he would not. He wanted her, and it had to be now. He slid her up the bed, hooked her leg around his and drove into her.

Last night had been slow and tender, but now there was an urgency—one Lavinia wasn't sure she could match—but there was also an intensity there that excited her, a loss of control in this guarded man as he bucked inside her, an instant need that from nowhere somehow her body easily met in a storm not building but hitting, spreading from her centre and outwards, and she clung onto his shoulders and gripped with her legs, bit on her lip to stay quiet.

He could feel her dense orgasm capture his, felt the shatter of release as he entered a place he had never sought, as he drove hard within her. He could hear her calling his name, and he was saying hers too.

They coupled.

It was a word he had never considered, never used, but in the midst of orgasm its meaning was crystal-clear—so clear he could actually *see* its meaning, feel her vibrations match his as she pulled him deep into her centre. He felt her fading twitches massage the last throes from him and he did not want it to be over, still lingering even after his body was spent. He lay on top of her for a moment, and her hands were still on his back. Zakahr wanted to recoil, to climb off, to get out—because the intimacy was killing him, because somehow he had to detach. And yet *still* he lingered, still his body refused to obey his demand, still he kissed, still he was inside her—still she was in his head. And somehow, if he was to keep her for a little while longer, he had to trust her.

'We should get up for breakfast…' She lay in his arms, unfazed by his silence. 'When do we leave?'

'In a couple of hours.'

She picked up his wrist and glanced at his watch. 'This time tomorrow I'll be back at my desk,' Lavinia grumbled.

Maybe this wouldn't be so hard after all, he decided. Maybe this was what she'd intended.

'Why not take some time off?' Zakahr said. 'Concentrate on getting Rachael.' He saw just a smudge of a frown. 'You could stay with me…'

'Sorry?'

'Move in with me.'

Lavinia laughed—she just laughed.

'I'm serious. You just said you don't—'

'It was a comment, Zakahr. I was grumbling about

work—not fishing. Why would you ask me to move in? Any day now I could be guardian to—'

'Just for a while.' He saw the smile wobble, made himself say it. 'Till I return to the UK.'

And she'd known she could never keep him, had accepted as best she could that it could never last, but did he have to remind her so soon? She tried to sound casual, tried not to reveal that her heart was breaking. 'And who's going to do my job if I suddenly leave?'

'You don't have to worry about that,' he said evenly. 'I called Abigail, my PA, on Friday. She should be there by tomorrow.'

'Oh, but I do worry.' She sat up, pulling up her knees and whipping the sheet tightly around her, hating how easily she was being replaced. 'I like my job…' She shook her head. 'I *need* my job—I'm not leaving.'

'Lavinia, I tell you—you won't have to worry…' He reached out to caress her back, his fingers reaching for her shoulders, running the length of her prominent spine, glad now he hadn't signed that contract—righteous, even, in his decision. She *was* far better out of it. 'I like spending time with you—I want to spend time with you.' It was an extremely unusual admission from Zakahr. 'I'm trying to help…' He forced the words out. 'Soon there will be no job…'

She went to turn her head, but froze. Katina's bitter words, which he had dismissed so readily with his assurances, now repeating.

'You're going to destroy—'

'I'm closing it,' Zakahr interrupted.

'Destroying it.' Her lips were white. Hugging her

knees tighter, she curled up at the wretchedness of it, her mind full of Rachael, how her employment status might change things. If she did get custody, how was she supposed to support her? 'I can't believe you'd do this.' The implications were trickling in now—her colleagues, Nina. The ramifications grew bigger with each cascading thought.

'What about Jasmine…?' Lavinia was appalled. They were here as their guests, and Zakahr was planning on closing Kolovsky! 'She's getting married in a few weeks…'

'Lavinia—I've been doing this for a long time. People will be looked after—there will be redundancy packages, agreements reached. You cannot make this personal…'

'It *is* personal, though!' And she said the words she had the first day they had met. *'It's her wedding…'*

'Her father will be able to sort it… It's a dress…' This wasn't going as well as he had hoped, and he moved to calm her. 'You are going to be fine. You will be away from all the fall-out. You can stay with me, and I will make sure you don't have to look for another job. When I'm gone, you will be able to concentrate on just yourself and Rachael—you can do your studies…'

Her spine straightened beneath his touch, ramrod straight, and the muscles over her shoulders tensed rigid as he named a price—a price, Zakahr surmised, that was beyond her wildest dreams, that would secure her future, so of course she was silent—of course it was a shock. And then her head turned in fury, till the blue eyes that had always smiled darkened in fury.

'You'll *pay* me to be your mistress?'

'I want to look after you.'

'While you're here,' Lavinia snarled, 'you'll pay me to sleep with you.'

'You're twisting things.'

'I don't have to twist anything. It's pretty blatant.'

'This way—' Zakahr started. But Lavinia would not let him continue.

'This way I'll be your prostitute.'

'You're being ridiculous.'

'Actually, no. I'm an expert on the subject—my mother was a prostitute, Zakahr. I've done everything I can to claw my way out of that pit, and you'd hurl me straight back in…'

'I am offering you a chance to change your life.'

'For the greater good?' Lavinia scoffed. 'What happens in ten years, when the gas bill's late or Rachael needs schoolbooks? Will I justify it then? You're offering me money, and at the same time you've taken away everything special about last night.'

She wanted to spit at him, but she wouldn't lower herself. Zakahr had done that enough already. She was out of bed in a trice, jumping out as if it were on fire, and wrapped in a sheet she turned to him. 'I don't need your charity, Zakahr. In fact, you're the one I feel sorry for—the only way you can get affection is to pay for it!'

She would have loved to dress and leave, but there really was no easy escape given they were on a yacht— so Lavinia locked herself in the bathroom, showering away every trace of his scent, repulsed at what he had said and trying hard not to cry, trying to wash away all evidence of what had taken place. He could not possibly have shamed her more, and all Lavinia wanted was *out*.

Stepping out of the shower, she wrapped herself in a towel and wondered how she could go out there and face him—wondered how on earth she was supposed to face not just him, but Jasmine, the King. How she could ever go back to work knowing what was to come? She realised she would have to deal with this the only way she knew how.

He heard the shower turned off, waited for her to come out—except she was taking ages, and for once Zakahr did not know how he should react. Cursing his choice of words, but not the sentiment behind them, because he *did* want to take care of her, he was bristling, too—he did *not* have to pay for affection. Women threw themselves at him. And yet...

Zakahr closed his eyes. He neither wanted nor needed affection—did not want the questions that came with companionship. Rather, he preferred the detachment that money allowed. He lay, wondering how best to deal with Lavinia, which words might soothe, for already she knew far too much. He would comfort her, Zakahr decided, dry her tears—even apologise if he had to...

Except as the bathroom door opened and Lavinia came out he was stunned at what he saw.

There was no trace of tears, her hair was glossy and tied back in a low ponytail, her make-up was on and—most confusing of all—she smiled over to him and, without a trace of embarrassment or shame, dropped her towel and pulled on her underwear.

'You'd better get ready.'

In purple panties and bra she hurried him, and Zakahr watched as she put on a simple white cami, then topped it with a smart lilac trouser suit. She looked fresh and poised and incredibly beautiful, and—worse for Zakahr—she was still smiling.

Worse still, she was looking him straight in the eye.

He had expected tears, arguments, perhaps, even that she might have reconsidered—it was a life-changing sum, after all. But instead she was looking at him, smiling at him, talking to him as if none of it mattered, as if she was enjoying his company, even—and it hit him then like a fist in the stomach. She was performing—just as she had for those revolting men she had once danced for.

Lavinia—the real Lavinia he had started to glimpse—was closed.

CHAPTER THIRTEEN

'MORNING.' He walked in on Monday to the scent of freshly brewed coffee and pleasing perfume. The computers were on, as he sat at his desk his diary was open at today's page, his schedule updated, and of course there should be nothing but relief when he looked up and it wasn't Lavinia bringing him coffee but Abigail instead.

The journey back to Melbourne had been hellish. There had been no grand gestures, no flouncing off. Instead Lavinia had chatted away about nothing, thanked him when his car had dropped her off, and then walked up her garden path and closed her door.

She wouldn't be back—of that he was sure. And it was for the best, Zakahr told himself. For without Lavinia buzzing in his ear, messing with his head, finally he could execute his plans.

'I want this sorted by the end of the week,' Zakahr told Abigail.

'I thought we had longer.'

'I want it done,' Zakahr said—because he just wanted to be on that plane and heading home. But even his head protested at that word. Home? To where? London?

Switzerland? Or would he stop over in Singapore? Home to what? His family was here.

He *had* no family, Zakahr reminded himself.

'Aleksi Kolovsky called,' Abigail unwittingly taunted him. 'He says it's nothing urgent. He just called from his honeymoon to see how things were going.'

Zakahr shrugged and flicked his hand, which told Abigail to disregard it—that it wasn't important. They had worked together for years. Abigail was married— very happily married—which meant she would never jeopardise things with sudden demands. But they were still occasional lovers, and Zakahr could not fathom that now, even as Abigail flirted a little and offered him a cue.

'It seems a little strange…' Abigail smiled '…just us in Australia.'

'It won't be for long.' Zakahr did not pursue it. 'I'm making the announcement on Friday—you'll need to arrange the press—but till then try to keep it business as normal as far as you can. Though I *do* need the auditors in.' He recited his orders. 'I want the team flown in by the weekend. I'm leaving straight after the press conference on Friday.'

He saw Abigail frown. Normally Zakahr stayed to wrap things up, was steadfast in his decisions. He stood by the burning building as it fell, answered questions, and fended off the reporters.

'Won't you be needed here?' Abigail checked. 'At least for a few days?'

'I've been away long enough. It will be pure admin.'

He turned to his computer, and because she wasn't

Lavinia, Abigail took her cue. Did not question a detail, nor argue a point. But there was one thing he needed to clear up, so he headed out of his office, to where Abigail was now working, and briefly brought Abigail up to speed.

'There was an assistant,' Zakahr said. 'Lavinia. I doubt she will be back, but just in case, she is to know nothing…' His voice trailed off, for there she was, walking in, just as she had on that first day, offering a quick apology for being late and carrying a large takeaway coffee. Only this morning her make-up was fully on.

'*I'm* Lavinia.' She offered her hand to Abigail, who after a moment's hesitation shook it. 'Just ask me anything you need to know, or need me to do.' And, swishing past Zakahr with a bright smile, she wished him a good morning, then headed for her old office.

With that she set the tone.

It was business, but it was so not as normal—Lavinia was just caught up in the dance of pretence, while knowing it was all a charade. She loathed Abigail, with her pussy-cat smile and her long red nails that lingered too long on his arm—loathed the scent of the woman who was so devoted to Zakahr that she would accept him without question. Not that she let Abigail see how she felt.

'Rula's agent insists the new contract is signed before her client puts on weight.' Lavinia listened as Abigail passed on the message. 'They've drawn it up; I've got it here. I'll bring it through and let Katina know.'

'Here.' She made the other woman a drink, rolled

her eyes in sympathy as Abigail juggled with an angry Katina on the phone.

'He'll sign it soon,' Abigail said crisply to the chief designer, 'and we'll get it couriered. Go ahead with the alterations. One moment.' She handed a file to Lavinia. 'Could you ask Zakahr to sign these? He knows what it's about.' She returned her attention to the phone call with Katina. 'That's your department. Zakahr does not need to be concerned with those details.'

Zakahr didn't look up when the door was knocked upon and opened. Abigail had said she was bringing the documents in, but whether it was her scent, or her walk, or just her presence, before the paperwork even reached his desk he knew that it was Lavinia.

'These are for you to sign.'

He looked at her immaculate French polished nails, then dragged his eyes up past her immaculate clothes to her groomed face. There was no trace of tears, no malice in her eyes—there was nothing.

A nothing he wanted to refute—because he *knew* she was hurting.

She was unreadable, and that was what killed him— she was closed off to him, and he did not like it a bit. But he consoled himself that it was for the best—his plans were coming into place. Soon it would be done with—soon he could resume his life. If only Lavinia stopped challenging him. Zakahr had no conscience where his family were concerned, and he had considered it the same in business—figures, facts were what he dealt with. Numbers, the bottom line. It had to be that way—and yet a lowly assistant was like a loose cannon now, bursting into his office and asking for answers, her lips smiling but her blue eyes glinting with confrontation, forcing self-examination when Zakahr would rather not.

'Just one thing,' Lavinia said as he picked up his pen. 'If you do go ahead with your plans, just understand that with a stroke of your pen you're about to terminate her career.'

'Rula will get other work...'

'Rula will be known as the Face Kolovsky didn't want.' Lavinia tossed her hair. 'And thanks to this contract she'll be several kilos heavier!'

'She'll be all the healthier for it.' Zakahr signed with a flourish, but his teeth seemed welded together as he passed her the forms.

'Has she rung yet?' Lavinia asked, and Zakahr shook his head in impatience.

'Why would Rula ring *me*?'

'I meant Ms Hewitt,' Lavinia retorted—because even if it was hell right now, even if her heart was breaking, there were other more important things on her mind.

'No.'

'She did say that she would?' Lavinia checked, and for just a fraction the mask slipped. 'That wasn't another piece of your plan to get me away from this place?'

'No.' Zakahr almost tasted blood. It felt as if he were swallowing shards of glass as he heard her take on things. He could see how it looked—the night away, Abigail flying in... 'I will let you know when she calls.'

* * *

He didn't.

She limped through to Thursday, but it took every ounce of strength she possessed to go to work. She should just leave, just walk away. Except she wouldn't give him the satisfaction—and there was, despite all evidence to the contrary, still a flare of hope in her heart that Zakahr would not go through with it, that he would be the wonderful, intuitive man she knew he could be, the caring man who had listened about Rachael.

And the devil himself she was sure *did* have a conscience. Because while she smiled and carried on as before, while she made extra effort with her appearance, Zakahr didn't seem to care less. He'd stopped shaving—since Sydney his face had not met a razor—but unfortunately it made him look sexier.

What wasn't so endearing was that for the first time since he'd taken over Zakahr had the same suit on for a second day in a row—and, Lavinia was positive, the same shirt. And he wasn't wearing a tie.

She wondered whose bed he'd just rolled out of.

'I don't give "warm wishes".' He placed two letters she'd actually been asked to draft on her desk beside her, and Lavinia should have jumped—after all, she was scrolling through Positions Vacant—but she refused to jump to *him*.

'And I'm not a typist,' Lavinia said. 'What do you prefer—yours truly?'

The irony wasn't wasted on Zakahr, and he gave a thin smile. Even though they barely spoke, when they did, thanks to Lavinia—who had always refused to bend to him—they managed pretty much as before.

'Yours sincerely,' Zakahr said. 'If you can manage it.' He glanced at her computer screen. 'Anything good?'

'A few!' Lavinia said. 'Don't worry—I shan't ask for a reference.'

It shouldn't concern him at all. But as he sat later, going over and over the events of tomorrow with Abigail, over and over his mind drifted to Lavinia.

What would she do?

He'd seen the jobs she was looking at—and he knew the types of qualifications they required. She'd need a pretty good job to match her wage. She was, he admitted, one of the sharpest people he knew—but by her own admission on paper she was qualified for little.

It wasn't his problem.

He'd never have got where he was if he'd worried about individual staff—Zakahr had to be ruthless. He'd come from nothing. She could do it, too.

'Your mail.' Lavinia knocked and went in, handed him his personal mail—which was one of the few jobs still left to her.

'Thanks.' He didn't even look up at her, and Abigail sat in silence, clearly waiting for Lavinia to be gone.

'Oh, Abigail.' Lavinia smiled sweetly. 'The beauticians rang—they can squeeze you in for your Brazilian after all. Just so long as you don't need your bottom done! I said I wasn't sure, and that you'd call them back.'

'That was cruel.' Zakahr couldn't help but grin as a purple-faced Abigail excused herself for a moment.

'No,' Lavinia corrected, 'that was bliss!' She turned to go, but then, blonde, dizzy, still absolutely stunning, she turned back. 'I've just had Alannah on the phone. She's a bit upset there are internal auditors going into the boutique.'

'External,' Zakahr corrected. 'They're an international firm I regularly use. Just tell her something—I don't know.' He shrugged. 'Tell her I don't trust anyone else's figures—even Nina and Aleksi could not agree on Kolovsky's worth. Tell her there's nothing to worry about.'

'Lie to her?'

'It's your job to keep things normal,' Zakahr said. 'If you can't handle it…'

'Fine—I'll tell her. I'm going to the boutique anyway. Abigail's given me quite a shopping list!'

As Zakahr took a phone call, Lavinia flounced out. A boot-faced Abigail scowled at her from her desk.

'If you ever do that again…'

'You'll what?' Lavinia challenged. 'Fire me?'

'I'll speak to Zakahr!'

'And tell him what? That I'm a bitch?' Lavinia just laughed. 'Oh, I can be…'

Unfortunately Zakahr chose that moment to put in an appearance. 'Come,' he said. 'I'll speak to Alannah myself. You can have a lift.'

It was their first real time alone since the weekend, and for Zakahr, even if it was awkward, it was actually a relief to get out of the office. As they moved out of the city Zakahr watched as Lavinia looked out of the window. Perhaps feeling his eyes, Lavinia turned and gave him a smile. It didn't look false, and that was the part that gutted him—he knew it had to be.

'How are you doing?' he asked—because despite everything he did want to know.

'Good!' she said.

'Lavinia…' Zakahr could not stand the bright smile. 'Can you drop the act…?'

Never. She would smile, she would carry on, she would laugh and she would talk. But she would never let him in again.

'Ms Hewitt just called.' There was a slight inclination of her head. It was the only indication of how much this mattered to her. 'That is why I wanted you away from the office. I confirmed that you have worked for Kolovsky for more than two years…'

'Did you tell her that after tomorrow I wouldn't have a job?'

'Of course not.'

'She'll find out anyway.' Lavinia shrugged. 'I've got an appointment with her at lunchtime.'

'I told her that you are responsible—that you have…'

Except Lavinia shook her head—didn't need to hear it. Instead she opened the partition and chatted with Eddie about his tiny granddaughter.

When they got to the boutique she didn't wait for Eddie to come round and open the door—just shot out of the car and walked ahead of him. And it was Lavinia who held the heavy door open as Zakahr refused to hesitate. He had seen many House of Kolovsky boutiques on his travels, but he had never been able to bring himself to go in, loathing them from the outside.

'Age before beauty!' Lavinia said brightly—only today she didn't make him smile.

He was very good with Alannah and her team. Lavinia had to give credit where it was due. In fifteen minutes he had the worried staff convinced this audit was nothing out of the ordinary, that it would all take place after hours, and that none of the clients would know, nothing would be compromised.

Lavinia picked up Abigail's order, which was actually two dresses, a jacket and a sheer silk shirt, a thick coat, and a gorgeous heavy silk scarf that Lavinia could quite happily have throttled her with—because if it was worth a fortune today, as Abigail knew only too well, tomorrow it would be priceless.

As they went to walk out of the boutique, as always Lavinia's eyes lingered a moment on her favourite signature piece. He must have followed her gaze as Zakahr's hand moved to the garment and there was a flare of recognition in his eyes.

'*Koža*,' Lavinia said. 'This is what it looks like when it's made up—this is the one I was trying to explain.'

It was nothing more than a slip dress—really it should merit nothing more than a glance. Except Zakahr was for a moment mesmerised.

'How…?' The simple, albeit beautiful, cloth he had held in his fingers now hung ruched and softly fluted at the bottom. There was no zip that he could see, no darts, just one simple seam at the back and two thin straps.

'Magic,' Lavinia said. 'Which is another word for bias.' She watched him frown. 'Cross-grain?' she attempted, and now it was Lavinia who rolled her eyes. 'You really are a fashion virgin.'

'At least I don't pretend otherwise,' Zakahr said, and Lavinia's little smile of triumph faded, taken over by a blush.

'I don't have to pretend any more,' Lavinia said. 'Thanks to you!'

And he heard the implication of a future with another and Zakahr didn't like it. But Lavinia would not linger. Instead she turned her attention back to the slip dress.

'Ivan really was a genius.'

'What was he like?' Zakahr surprised himself by asking—but from Lavinia he knew he would hear part of the truth.

'A bully,' Lavinia responded instantly. 'He snapped his fingers and Nina jumped—everyone jumped. He loved his women; he flaunted them in her face. His latest mistress was even standing there with Nina at his deathbed…' She thought for a moment. 'Poor Nina.' She would *not* be silenced; she would always speak as she found. 'She used to be all bloated and miserable. I'm sure she drank—I'm sure he hit her…'

He wished she'd stop.

'But he *was* a genius.' She looked around the boutique at the amazing things his twisted mind had created. 'And, God help her, Nina loved him.'

They walked out of the boutique to the waiting limousine, and as Eddie waited for a suitable gap in the traffic Zakahr looked at the familiar cerulean blue building. There should be triumph building, surely? Except when he turned away he saw Lavinia staring at the building too, a faraway look in her eyes, and he remembered their first journey and how different things had been.

Her phone bleeped and she read a text message. For a second she closed her eyes, and then gave a wry smile. 'Jasmine.'

Just for a moment he swore he saw a flash of tears in her eyes, and Zakahr knew that despite the smile and the talk and the clothes she was struggling inside. He did the kindest thing he could.

'I won't be needing you tomorrow.'

She was silent for a moment before she spoke. 'Am I just to watch it on the news?'

'Resign,' Zakahr said. 'I'll ensure you get a good package.' He saw the clench of her jaw and corrected himself. 'A fair package. You can say you were so opposed when you found out that you resigned on principle…'

It was actually a relief.

There was sadness—an aching sadness—but there was actually relief.

'Can I come back for my things this afternoon?'

'Of course.'

'Can you be out?'

It killed her that he nodded.

CHAPTER FOURTEEN

THIS had nothing to do with Zakahr.

She sat in Ms Hewitt's cluttered office and, though her world was falling apart, she knew she couldn't blame this part of it on him.

'Your references are wonderful,' Ms Hewitt said. 'Lavinia, I am so impressed at how you have turned your life around, and I don't doubt you would be a wonderful carer for Rachael. But we go to every length to keep a family together, and with extra support we feel Rachael…'

Lavinia had begged and pleaded her case, all to no avail, and now it came down to this. 'Will I still get to see her?'

'Of course.' Ms Hewitt was the kindest she had been. 'I've spoken to Rowena and suggested you have time with her this afternoon, and I've also recommended in my report that you have overnight access once a week— which is more than before. Your role as a big sister to Rachael is one we take seriously.'

'And the decision is made?'

'There'll be a case conference on Monday,' Ms Hewitt said. 'I just wanted to tell you what to expect.'

'Is there anything I can do?'

'Lavinia…' Ms Hewitt took off her glasses. 'You can get a lawyer—you can challenge things, delay things a little—but nobody is on trial here. It's not about winning or losing. It's about what's best for Rachael.'

She *was* what was best for Rachael.

Despite the decision, right at her very core Lavinia knew that.

And she would be a good parent; the next hour proved that—because, even though she was bleeding inside, she fronted up to the hardest gig of her life and smiled when she collected Rachael.

'Where are we going?' Rachael asked as Lavinia started the car.

'We have to go to my office, just so I can collect a few things,' Lavinia said. There were essentials there, like her make-up bag and her MP3 player, but hopefully Zakahr wouldn't be there—still, given the hour, she thought it better to warn Rachael.

'My boss might be a bit funny,' Lavinia explained as they parked the car and walked along the city street and through the golden doors. 'He's a bit of a grump—and you wait till you meet Abigail.' She pulled a face, which involved making her eyes go crossed. Unfortunately at the same time the lift doors opened. Unfortunately Zakahr was in the lift.

His eyes looked to Rachael, and then away.

He did not want to see her—did not want to think of what he was doing to either of them.

Could not.

He could feel Rachael's eyes on him, wished the lift would go faster.

'Is that your boss?' Rachael asked, and Lavinia's eyes widened a fraction. Rachael rarely initiated conversation, and Lavinia rather wished she hadn't chosen now to start.

'It is,' Lavinia said.

'The grumpy one?' Rachael checked, and without looking Lavinia just knew Zakahr's tongue was rolling in his cheek.

They did a little dance as he went to step out. Zakahr was desperate to get out of the confines of the lift, but then he remembered his manners—though he wished he hadn't, because now he had to walk behind them.

See more of them.

Lavinia, polished and glamorous. Rachael, her dark curls in knots, her socks grubby and mismatched, wearing a T-shirt too short and shorts too long. He could see why Lavinia was upset that the clothing she bought for her sister wasn't being passed on to the little girl.

He just didn't *want* to see.

'I won't be long. I just need to get my things,' Lavinia said as they reached the office.

Zakahr brushed past without response.

'Right, can you sit there for five minutes? I just need to empty out my desk,' Lavinia said as brightly as she could as Rachael sat on the sofa.

For Zakahr it was hell.

Zakahr's job meant *not* getting involved.

Figúres he could deal with—sob-stories he just tuned out.

For his business to survive he had to be ruthless.

He did not *want* to know about Eddie and his sick grandchild, he did not *want* to know that Lavinia's mortgage was a monthly concern, and more than that, he did not *want* a face to the name of Rachael.

Zakahr stared unseeing out of his office window, tried to tell himself that this time tomorrow he would be on a plane, that all he was leaving behind was not his problem.

Yet it wasn't that which consumed him.

Somehow—even though he had deliberately not thought about it, had done his level best not to think about it—somehow he had pictured Rachael as a mini-Lavinia. A blonde, precocious child—a resilient, happy little thing. What had shocked him to the core—what he was having so much trouble dealing with at this very moment—was that Rachael reminded Zakahr of himself.

He could feel her mistrust, her fear, her resignation, her expectation that hurt would follow hurt.

He could not stand to be involved.

He did not want to be involved.

He gave millions to charity, he spoke at functions—but there were no pictures of Zakahr donning a baseball cap and smiling beside a child. He kept his distance.

He was being manipulated, he was sure.

Deliberately not thinking, certainly for once not analysing, he pressed on the intercom.

'Lavinia?' When she didn't come immediately, he marched out of the office. 'Can I see you now?'

'One moment.' She was getting Rachael a drink from

the water cooler, refusing to let him rush her, and Zakahr returned to his office, sat at his desk. Ages later, but more like a moment, she came in.

'Is this the sympathy card you're playing?' Zakahr challenged as soon as the door was closed. 'Because if you're using her...'

'*I'm* not the one who uses people, Zakahr.' Lavinia was as direct as ever. 'And just in case that black heart of yours is having an attack of guilt, though I doubt it, there's no need. I didn't get access to Rachael, so my lack of a job doesn't affect her future one bit. Now, if you'll excuse me, I need to get my things.'

'She's going back?'

'Yep!'

Lavinia shrugged, but Zakahr could see the effort behind the apparent nonchalance. It was as if her shoulders were pushing up bricks.

'She'll adapt. Oh, and Zakahr...' She gave him a black smile. 'On the drive here I heard them announce tomorrow's press conference on the radio. Enjoy your revenge—hope it's everything you've dreamed of.'

'What did you expect, Lavinia?' He could see that she didn't get it. 'Did you really think that I'd come here to make things up with my family? Have you any idea—?'

'I've got a perfectly good idea of what you must have gone through,' Lavinia shouted. 'Because I lived it, Zakahr—because so many times I wished that my mother had turned her back on *me*. The same way I wish Rachael's father would turn her back on *her*.'

'What Nina did—'

'I'll tell you what she did,' Lavinia said, 'this woman you hate so much. She did something she bitterly regrets—has done many things she no doubt bitterly regrets. But she will always be my friend.'

'Your *friend*?'

'My friend,' Lavinia admitted. 'She gave me a decent job, gave me a chance in life. I didn't just dream of weddings, Zakahr. I used to lie in bed at night, listening to my mum entertaining her *friends*, and wish that I'd find out I was adopted. To this day sometimes I wish my mother had done what Nina did. Believe me, sometimes I think it would have been kinder.'

'Well, I think that rules out a career in counselling!' Lavinia said to a nonplussed Rachael, and then she kissed her nose—whether Rachael wanted it or not.

'Love you,' Lavinia said, and kissed her little fat cheek, which was probably the wrong thing too. But there was almost a smile on Rachael's cross little face. 'I love you so much.' Which was, no doubt, according to Ms Hewitt, putting too much pressure on her. But Rachael was smiling, and Lavinia gave her a little tickle, and then she was actually laughing. 'I want to eat you up, you're so cute.'

And it was so nice to just be sisters—one big, one little, one funny, one serious, but sisters.

And they *should* be together.

Ignoring potential wrath, Lavinia didn't take Rachael for a milkshake or a boring swing in the park, and neither did she take her back to Rowena straight away.

'Where are we going?' Rachael stood on the elevator in a large department store as they went up past children's wear, past toys, past books, till finally they were in the bedding department.

'We need to sort out your room,' Lavinia said, trying to work out how much room she had left on her credit card. 'Let's choose some nice bedclothes.'

'Am I coming to live with you?' Rachael asked, and Lavinia could hear the hope and fear and doubt in her sister's voice. It almost broke her heart that she couldn't give the answer they both surely wanted.

'Not for now,' Lavinia admitted. 'But I'm going to keep trying to make that happen. I don't get to decide…' She saw Rachael's little pinched face tighten. 'But you *are* going to have your own room at my house.' Then she qualified it a touch. 'Wherever I live there will be a room there for you—even if I can only get you one night now and then, or even if we have to wait till you're sixteen.' Lavinia had an appalling thought. 'I'll be in my thirties!' She was surprised that Rachael actually smiled. 'Come on.'

It was, in spite of a broken heart, in spite of losing everything dear to her, one of the best hours of her life.

She didn't listen to the experts, she listened to her heart—and, yes, it was Zakahr's advice she took.

They chose pinks and greens for her bedspread and pillowcases, and a butterfly dreamcatcher, and then Lavinia got Rachael the cheapest mobile phone. They took their wares *home*, and made up the bed and put up curtains, and Lavinia set up the phone and taught Rachael how to text.

X

'I'll send you a kiss every night,' Lavinia said. 'And, if you can, you can send me one back.'

So Rachael had a go at texting, and Lavinia's phone bleeped, and she got her first kiss from Rachael.

'Come on,' Lavinia said. 'Let's get you back to Rowena.'

And this time when she offered her hand Rachael took it.

'You know, we're going to be okay,' Lavinia said. 'I'm going to make sure of it.'

And she did try to hand her back with grace—did her absolute best to trust that Ms Hewitt maybe did know best—but as they walked up the garden path Lavinia could feel her heart cracking as Rachael looked up at her.

'I want to be with you.'

'You'll be fine,' Lavinia said as bravely as she could. She saw Rowena's shadow as she came to open the door, and then her heart surely stopped beating.

'Lavinia, I don't want to go back to him.'

And she knew you should never make a child promises you couldn't keep but, handing her over to Rowena, Lavinia hugged her tight and made one. 'I'll do everything I can.'

'Promise?'

Lavinia nodded. 'I promise.'

She let her go, smiled to Rowena and even managed

a wave as she drove off. But hearing Rachael's plea was more than she could bear, because on Monday she *was* going back to her father.

There wasn't time to break down, there wasn't time to cry, there really wasn't much time to think.

All Lavinia knew was that she'd do anything for that little girl.

Anything.

CHAPTER FIFTEEN

SHE could do this, Lavinia told herself.

Lavinia paced the city streets, high heels clicking, and she didn't care.

Kevin wanted money, a significant amount of money, and she knew where she could get it. She just had to work out how.

There was the Kolovsky boutique—the place every woman wanted to be—and she stared in at the window and saw the silk and the opals. And then she saw her reflection, and it would have been so easy to rest her head on the window and just weep, but if she started she would never stop. Instead she swept into the store and selected a Kolovsky wrap—one of the last designs of the founder, Ivan Kolovsky, spun in golds and reds and ambers, in the same thread as the dress she had worn that night she had first kissed Zakahr. The staff knew her, of course, but they blinked a little when she told them to charge it to Zakahr Belenki.

'And this, too,' Lavinia informed them, grabbing a *koža* slip dress. And then she saw another wrap, a turquoise one, filled with silvers and greens like a peacock on display, and she knew who would love this one.

Ignoring Alannah's incessant questions and requests for a signature, Lavinia left—and ground the gears in her car all the way to the hospital.

'Here.' She wrapped it round Nina's shoulders. 'Ivan designed this one.' She smoothed the silk around her friend's shoulders and tried to comfort her. But she wouldn't stop crying, wouldn't stop wailing.

'He's called a press conference for tomorrow. It's over,' Nina sobbed. 'Tomorrow it is all over.'

'Stop it,' Lavinia said, because it was too much like her own mother.

'He hasn't been in to see me. He'll never forgive me. Riminic won't come to see me.' Round and round on the same pointless loop. 'He's never going to forgive me.'

'Perhaps not!' Lavinia was cross, but she was kind. 'Maybe he'll never forgive you, Nina. But you know what? You can forgive yourself. You did a terrible, awful thing—but that's not all you are. You've done many good things, too—look how you helped me. You gave me a good job, you helped me with Rachael, with so many things.'

'I want my son.'

'You *have* your son!' Lavinia said. 'Whether he forgives you, or loves you, still you have your son…' But there was no reaching her, and the doctor moved in with medication. Lavinia shooed him off. 'You want more Valium, Nina? Or why not have a drink, like my mum did? Or you can get up, get washed…'

'It hurts,' Nina insisted, thumping at her chest, and Lavinia couldn't do it any more.

'*Life* hurts,' Lavinia said. 'But you can't just give in.

Sometimes you do what you have to at the time, and then work out how to forgive yourself afterwards.'

And so, now, must she.

For the first time in almost a week Zakahr shaved. He stood with a towel around his hips and tried somehow to shave and not fully look at himself in the mirror.

His suit was chosen for the morning, his speech written, his case packed. Soon it would be over.

And then came a frantic knocking at his door.

'Yes?'

Zakahr stood back as a mini-torpedo swept into his suite.

'I've changed my mind.' She was breathless, could not look at him, but she was determined. 'That offer.'

'What offer?'

'For money.'

'Lavinia…' he sounded bored '…you told me very clearly that money was the last thing you wanted.'

'I've changed my mind.' There was a frantic air to her, an urgency as she rained his face with kisses.

'Lavinia…'

Zakahr peeled her off him. He did not want to deal with this. He did not want to deal with *her*, Lavinia, the person who made him sway, this woman who clouded his judgment. So he pushed her away with words.

'I might have known you'd revert to type.'

'I'm my mother's daughter.'

'Just go.'

She could not. She would not.

So she did it—she pulled off her dress to reveal the

koža slip beneath. She was shaking, and ashamed, but worse—far worse—he remained unmoved.

'Here.' He strode across the room to his desk, pulled out a cheque. 'For the other night. Now, get out.'

And she had what she wanted, there in her hand, but it wasn't enough. It could never be enough—and it had nothing to do with money. She was kissing him again, pressing her lips on his unwilling mouth. He turned his face away.

'Is it money you want, Lavinia, or sex?' He wanted *her*, not what she was doing. He remembered her abhorrence at the idea and tried to save her from herself. Pulling at her wrists, he pushed her away from his body. For even as he rejected her she would surely be able to feel he was lying.

Both, she almost sobbed. But that wasn't the entire answer. There was a third—an addition that she could not bring herself to admit.

She didn't want him to go, yet somehow had to accept there was nothing here for him to stay for.

He had taken her heart—he might just as well have had the butler pack it amongst his shirts—and the fire died in her.

'What do you want, Lavinia?'

'Not this,' Lavinia admitted, and she stared at the cheque and then handed it to him. 'Thank you.'

'For what.'

'For not letting me...' She screwed her eyes closed. 'Please—just take it.'

He didn't.

'I don't want to make money this way—and the stupid

thing is you're the only man I could have tried to… I'm so ashamed.'

'You didn't do anything.'

'Not for that…' When still he wouldn't take the cheque she screwed it up in her hands. 'I promised myself I'd do anything it took to get Rachael, but in the end…'

'You don't need that money,' Zakahr said—which was great, coming from a billionaire.

She picked up her dress, and it was an almost impossible task to get out with dignity. But as she stepped into her shoes, rejected and broke, Lavinia was the one who could look him in the eye.

'I thought I wanted you…' She shook her head. 'But I don't. I want a family for Rachael—I want cousins and grandparents and brothers and sisters and aunts and uncles for her. I want everything for her that I never had, and everything you so readily could.'

She went to open the door. She knew she often said the wrong thing, but sometimes she couldn't stop herself, and now it was building and fizzing and welling inside her, and she probably wouldn't have said it if the damn door hadn't stuck.

'So you were abandoned?' Lavinia finally wrenched the door open, turned around and stuck her chin out to him. 'Boo-hoo—get over it.'

And, in high stilettos and a *koža* slip, she marched right out of his life.

CHAPTER SIXTEEN

IT WAS his longest night.

He drove first to the hospital, sitting outside, knowing it was too late to go in. Then he drove to Iosef's home and watched the lights flick on and off—even heard the baby crying at midnight in the dark, silent street and saw the light flick on again. Then to Annika—a sister he had hardly spoken to. He sat outside the sprawling farm she shared with her husband Ross, listening to the horses and the peace and wishing it might come to his soul.

It could.

Well, according to Lavinia.

She'd taken thirty-six years of history, challenged a lifelong dream and told him he could do it.

'You don't need money.'

He'd leant on her doorbell till she answered, still in the *koža* slip, nursing a tub of ice cream and a glass of wine. Somehow, he could tell she had not been crying.

'I had already arranged a lawyer for you. He will contact you.'

'He rang before,' Lavinia said, and taking that phone

call had felt a whole lot different from taking money. 'He seems to think I have a good chance.'

'You have *every* chance,' Zakahr said.

He walked into her house and it was the first time he had felt at home.

There were her stolen goods all over the sofa, and a make-up bag on the coffee table, and a woman who somehow reached him.

'How am I supposed to forgive her? How can I stay...?'

'You choose to.' She smiled at him, but it was a tired one. 'She was fifteen,' Lavinia said, pouring him a glass of wine. She had listened to Nina's grief for so long now she knew her story by heart. 'She was scared and pregnant and they hid it from everyone. She was poor, his family would have been angry, and Ivan told her they could not keep you.'

She didn't elaborate on that part—they both knew the consequences.

'For years they were apart. Ivan had a fling with a cleaner—that was Levander's mother—then he met your mother again. She was nineteen then, and soon pregnant with twins. His family still objected to the marriage— she was beneath him, they said. She tried very hard to show them she was better, and she did not see how they would accept her if they knew there had already been a child. You would have been four.'

She tried to picture him at four, but it didn't make her smile.

'There was a chance to flee Russia. She was heavily pregnant, and Levander's mother came to the door, begging that they take him. Nina did not want Levander if she could not have her own son.'

He looked at Lavinia and her eyes were clear, her words very definite.

'I'm sorry.'

And she was. It wasn't her fault, it had nothing to do with her, but sorry she was as she told him his history.

'How did you forgive *your* mother?'

'I don't know that I actually did—I just gave up trying to change her. Can you forgive Nina?' Lavinia asked—because now she'd stopped being angry she knew it was a big ask.

'She really helped you?' Zakahr answered in question.

'They all have.' Lavinia nodded. 'They've been like a family.' She thought for a moment, because again she'd probably said the wrong thing. 'Not a lovey-dovey family—we fight all the time...'

'A real family, I guess.'

Zakahr closed his eyes. He would wear every scar on his back easier knowing that Nina had in some way been there for her.

'I love you,' he said. And he'd never thought he'd say it—and neither had Lavinia—and now to hear it, to know it, to feel it, for once she was lost for words. He could not gauge her silence, but if he had to make it clearer then he would. 'I'm crazy about you. So crazy all I can think of is you. So crazy I would give up a lifetime's revenge to have you.'

And then she climbed on his knee and kissed him—a bold kiss, a loving kiss, a Lavinia kiss, that started on his mouth and then moved across his cheeks and over his eyebrows. Her thin fingers roamed his hair. He knew this was a for ever he had never—not once—let himself glimpse. He could be himself. The past wasn't something he ran from or something that ate him up with a need to avenge. The past could just *be*, and that meant he now had a future.

It was a kiss that was both passionate and loving—a kiss that was both urgent and patient. She felt the exhaustion as his past left him, and the hope as the future greeted him, and it was a different kiss too, for Lavinia.

She tasted his tongue, and the lips that were designed for her. She wasn't unsure and she wasn't shy and she knew with him she was revered.

She straddled him and kissed him as his hands caressed her body through the silk. He kissed her breasts through the fabric his father had created, and then his mouth moved lower still, and she felt him, warm through the fabric. He kissed her stomach and slid the fabric up over her hips. She knelt on him till it was her flesh his lips were touching, and he kissed her stomach deeply as her fingers pressed in his hair. It was a kiss that told her his babies would grow there.

She slid down his zipper and lowered herself onto him, and it was third time lucky for Lavinia, because this time *she* got to love *him*.

She got to kiss him as he came deep within her. She got to kiss him as her body learnt how readily available true passion was. Because it was fast and intense and incredibly beautiful—a lot like life.

'Marry me,' he said because he wanted her for

ever. He kissed her again, and then asked her again.
'Marry me.'

'On one condition.'

She whispered it into his ear.

He'd have agreed to anything—just not that.

He closed his eyes, because it was impossible, but how
could he ever say no to her? He was still within her, and
he could never deny her. And then he opened them, and
saw that Lavinia was absolutely and completely serious
in her 'one condition'.

Hesitantly he agreed. Tonight could only be for ever
if he would do this for her. Then this love would be for
keeps.

Everyone would just have to wait till the wedding to
find out.

EPILOGUE

LAVINIA had no shame.

She *was* the bride-to-be from hell, and she didn't care who knew it.

As a child she had fallen asleep dreaming of this day, had blocked out the noises from the bedroom next door with dreams of her prince, and quite simply it had to be perfect.

Perfect! she informed each Kolovsky in turn.

If they couldn't move on or get along then she didn't want them at her wedding—and that included Zakahr.

The brothers would wear matching Kolovsky silk ties, and so too would Ross, Annika's husband. Annika and Nina were to wear shoes in the same silk.

'It's too much!' Katina grumbled. 'You need *subtle*— let us do what we do best.'

'It's *my* wedding!' Lavinia insisted.

And it was.

The dress that had waited to be worn by a Kolovsky bride and had been shunned each time was taken out of the display cabinet and fitted for Lavinia, and it was absolutely the best dress in the world.

She could feel the jewels in the hem that had been sewn in by Ivan.

Opal earrings from Nina dangled at her ears.

And she wore her mother's watch. It was the one thing Fleur had refused to pawn, a gift from her favourite client who, Lavinia had secretly dreamed, was maybe, just maybe, her father. Today she felt so sure and complete that Lavinia was quite certain he was.

'Big breaths,' said Hannah, the Salvation Army worker who had always been there for her while she grew up, and who would give her away on her biggest day.

'Are they all there?' Lavinia begged—because she wanted each and every one of the Kolovskys to share this.

She loved them all, every depraved, debauched, reformed one of them, and this day was not perfect without them all here.

'Levander's there,' Hannah said, peering into the church. Levander was easily spotted, because Zakahr had chosen him as his best man—two Detsky Dom boys made good, thanks to love.

'I'm here,' Annika, who was bridesmaid, pointed out. 'And I've seen Aleksi and Iosef go in.'

'And they're standing with Nina?' Lavinia checked.

'They are,' Annika said. 'You can stop worrying now.'

And she did. Standing at the doors of the church, it dawned on Lavinia that she could stop worrying now.

Zakahr had been right. Kevin had refused the DNA test Lavinia's lawyer had suggested. Rachael was not even his. And now the little girl was getting used to her new family. Too shy to be a bridesmaid, today she was being held by a doting Nina, and that serious face more often these days broke into a smile.

'You look wonderful,' Annika said to Lavinia, and it felt strange for Annika. She should be jealous—after all, her mother was so close to Lavinia—but how could she be jealous of a woman who had healed such a fractured family? 'You *are* wonderful,' Annika said, which was terribly effusive for her. And what was more she gave Lavinia a kiss.

The walk up the aisle was up to that moment the best walk of her life. But Lavinia wanted to gallop—because she wanted to walk back down it with *him*.

Zakahr smiled when he saw her—a smile that came from his soul. Because, unlike his sister and brothers, he knew her truth. His secret virgin walked towards him, and never till then had Zakahr considered himself lucky. But resentment was a memory now. His soul was devoid of anything bitter, and every piece of his past was worth it for this moment—because without pain he would not have recognised such joy.

Yes, he knew her truth, and she knew his—knew every story behind every scar—and still, steadfastly, she loved him.

Which was why he would do anything for her.

'You look beautiful,' he said when she joined him.

'I know!' Lavinia beamed and kissed him. 'So do you.'

There was a lot of talking, and a bit of singing—only

Lavinia didn't really hear it, because they were getting to the part that mattered the most, and her heart was hammering, and her hands were shaking.

He took them in his as he offered her his vows. And he held them and remembered what she'd whispered in his ear the night he'd asked her to marry him.

He could see his dazzling, happy wife, perhaps the strongest woman he knew, for the first time ever crying as Zakahr opened his mouth. Lavinia was crying because she knew how hard this was for him, but she knew, absolutely, that he could do it.

And he did.

'I, Zakahr Riminic Kolovsky…'

She heard the gasp from the congregation, turned and saw Nina holding Rachael, crying and smiling, and all his brothers and his sister standing proud.

She could only love him more as she stumbled through her own vows.

It was the most wonderful party.

The press were baying at the door, a helicopter hovered overhead, but no one inside cared. There was love in the air, and plenty to go around, and Lavinia danced and chatted and ate, and insisted everyone danced some more.

No, Zakahr did not dance with Nina, but they shared a drink and admired Lavinia—the one solid link between them.

Forgiveness wasn't a place Zakahr had arrived at yet, but he was making the journey. And if it was hard, still it brought rewards—there were enough Kolovskys to ensure he had far fewer trips to the airport!

'I never want to take it off!' She stood in the honeymoon suite and couldn't bear to take off the dress, just twirled at the mirror as Zakahr lay on the bed and watched.

Then she turned sideways and ran her hands over her latest phantom pregnancy, pressed in the fabric in a search for changes.

Zakahr suppressed a smile—she wasn't even late yet, though Lavinia insisted she felt bloated.

'Can we have lots of babies?'

'Lots,' Zakahr said. 'All boys!' Because he'd have his work cut out keeping tabs on mini-Lavinias.

Lavinia smiled and thought of lots of little grey-eyed, dark-haired boys, and gave a smile for the little girls she'd make sure they had too. 'I want a big family.'

'We've suddenly got one!' he said as she came over.

Lavinia held up her hair as Zakahr took care of a long row of buttons, his mouth tracing her spine.

'They're *my* family, except I feel like I'm marrying into *yours*, Mrs Kolovsky.'

'Say it again.' She was shameless.

'Mrs Kolovsky,' Zakahr duly said as he peeled the bodice down. 'Mrs Lavinia Kolovsky.'

She made it easy to say—so easy to become the person he was born to be, the only man to change his name on his wedding day!

Then Zakahr stilled for a moment, realised she wasn't imagining things as he saw the unfamiliar swell in her pale flat breasts, saw the changes in her body that would change their future.

'What?' She smiled up at him.

'Everything,' Zakahr said. 'You're everything to me.'

A STORMY SPANISH SUMMER
by Penny Jordan

Duque Vidal y Salvadores hated Fliss Clairemont—but now he must help her claim her inheritance! As their attraction takes hold, can Vidal admit how wrong he's been about her…?

NOT A MARRYING MAN
by Miranda Lee

Billionaire Warwick Kincaid asked Amber Roberts to move in, but then became distant. Is her time up? The chemistry between them remains *white-hot* and Amber finds it hard to believe that her time with Warwick is *really* over…

SECRETS OF THE OASIS
by Abby Green

After giving herself to Sheikh Salman years ago, Jamilah Moreau's wedding fantasies were crushed. Then Salman spirits her off to a desert oasis and Jamilah discovers he still wants her!

THE HEIR FROM NOWHERE
by Trish Morey

Dominic Pirelli's world falls apart with the news that an IVF mix-up means a stranger is carrying his baby! Dominic is determined to keep waif-like Angelina Cameron close, but who will have custody of the Pirelli heir?

On sale from 18th February 2011
Don't miss out!

Available at WHSmith, Tesco, ASDA, Eason
and all good bookshops
www.millsandboon.co.uk

MODERN

TAMING THE LAST ST CLAIRE
by Carole Mortimer

Gideon St Claire's life revolves around work, so fun-loving Joey McKinley is the sort of woman he normally avoids! Then an old enemy starts looking for revenge and Gideon's forced to protect Joey—day *and* night…

THE FAR SIDE OF PARADISE
by Robyn Donald

A disastrous engagement left Taryn wary of men, but Cade Peredur stirs feelings she's never known before. However, when Cade's true identity is revealed, will Taryn's paradise fantasy dissolve?

THE PROUD WIFE
by Kate Walker

Marina D'Inzeo is finally ready to divorce her estranged husband Pietro—even a summons to join him in Sicily won't deter her! However, with his wife standing before him, Pietro wonders why he ever let her go!

ONE DESERT NIGHT
by Maggie Cox

Returning to the desert plains of Kabuyadir to sell its famous *Heart of Courage* jewel, Gina Collins is horrified the new sheikh is the man who gave her one earth-shattering night years ago.

On sale from 4th March 2011
Don't miss out!

Available at WHSmith, Tesco, ASDA, Eason and all good bookshops

www.millsandboon.co.uk

2 FREE BOOKS
AND A SURPRISE GIFT

We would like to take this opportunity to thank you for reading this Mills & Boon® book by offering you the chance to take TWO more specially selected books from the Modern™ series absolutely FREE! We're also making this offer to introduce you to the benefits of the Mills & Boon® Book Club™—

- **FREE home delivery**
- **FREE gifts and competitions**
- **FREE monthly Newsletter**
- **Exclusive Mills & Boon Book Club offers**
- **Books available before they're in the shops**

Accepting these FREE books and gift places you under no obligation to buy, you may cancel at any time, even after receiving your free books. Simply complete your details below and return the entire page to the address below. You don't even need a stamp!

YES Please send me 2 free Modern books and a surprise gift. I understand that unless you hear from me, I will receive 4 superb new books every month for just £3.30 each, postage and packing free. I am under no obligation to purchase any books and may cancel my subscription at any time. The free books and gift will be mine to keep in any case.

Ms/Mrs/Miss/Mr _____ Initials _____

Surname _____

Address _____

_____

_____ Postcode _____

E-mail _____

Send this whole page to: Mills & Boon Book Club, Free Book Offer, FREEPOST NAT 10298, Richmond, TW9 1BR

Offer valid in UK only and is not available to current Mills & Boon Book Club subscribers to this series. Overseas and Eire please write for details.. We reserve the right to refuse an application and applicants must be aged 18 years or over. Only one application per household. Terms and prices subject to change without notice. Offer expires 30th April 2011. As a result of this application, you may receive offers from Harlequin Mills & Boon and other carefully selected companies. If you would prefer not to share in this opportunity please write to The Data Manager, PO Box 676, Richmond, TW9 1WU.

Mills & Boon® is a registered trademark owned by Harlequin Mills & Boon Limited.
Modern™ is being used as a trademark. The Mills & Boon® Book Club™ is being used as a trademark.